# THE CLOCK

*Clairvoyant Serial - Book 2*

## KATHRYN WISE

Soul Words

# CONTENTS

# FROM KATHRYN WISE

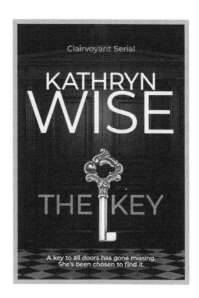

In the off chance you haven't read *The Key*, the first install-ment of the Clairvoyant Serial, you really must read it before you start *The Clock*.

**Go get it!**

It's forever .99, but if for some reason you don't want to purchase the book, I'm offering another option. If you sign up for my regular newsletter, I'll send you *The Key* FREE. Details can be found in the back of the book.

# PREVIOUSLY...FROM THE KEY

J ack Trader sat at the head of the table opposite the grand entry doors. Behind him a media curtain had been hung, as if there were plans for a presentation to be delivered later on. The room was otherwise vacant, leaving it cavernous and cold. Rachel and Grayson had arrived a few minutes before, quickly clearing security and then suffering the irritating slowness of the elevator. Grayson was in *Michael Raphael* mode, but on the short trip to the building, he had warned her of the change in format. The first 30 minutes would be with Mr. Trader. Alone.

"Good morning Michael. Thank you for escorting Ms. Wheaton again. And thank you as well for chiming in yesterday about needing to take a break. In retrospect, that was a good call on your part."

"Thanks, Jack. Anything for *Virtual Life*," Grayson said, flashing an upbeat smile.

"And good morning to you Ms. Wheaton. You look refreshed. I trust you're ready to proceed with the interview?"

"Why yes Mr. Trader. I am completely refreshed and ready to proceed. Thank you so much for your gracious flexibility. I've had time to prepare and look forward to spending more time with your team." Rachel sat down in the chair at the opposite head of the table from Trader. Grayson sat a few chairs down from her. "I understand you've decided to spend the first 30 minutes without your management team in attendance?"

"Oh yes. I sometimes like to have one-on-one time with key candidates; you know...to help them along. We have a very diverse group of heavy hitters on my team and sometimes their personalities can be...oh, how shall I say...off-putting?"

"I see. So you're going to give me some tips?"

"Um...in a manner of speaking. I want to introduce you to someone."

"I see. Of course. Whatever you think is best," Rachel said. She noticed Grayson shifting in his chair. Apparently, this was a surprise.

Rachel's internal alarm went off. She felt a new tension in the room.

First, there were the sounds.

The click of a closing door.

The sound of spike heels on a tile floor.

And the whoosh of a fabric curtain opening.

Mr. Trader rose from his chair.

Through the media curtain a woman appeared.

Mr. Trader cleared his throat. "I would like to introduce Ms. Veronica Priestly, one of our newest stars on the team."

There she was, standing in all of her *Cruella de Vil* splendor, dressed to the nines from head to toe.

And hanging from a simple chain around her neck…a blindingly brilliant platinum key.

# THE CLOCK

"There is another kind of time that the Greeks also named. *Kairos. While chronos refers to chronological or sequential time, man-made time, kairos signifies a time in-between, an uncounted moment in which something outside of chronos happens…In the New Testament, kairos is used when referring to the moment that fulfills the purpose of God, the moment God acts.*"[1]

[1]*Praying the Hours in Ordinary Life: (Art for Faith's Sake)*
*Lauralee Farrer and Clayton J. Schmit*

## Chapter One

# THE GAME'S AFOOT

Grayson was stern, his affable demeanor dissolving into a tense sobriety. Rachel forced a polite smile, pretending not to recognize the woman who'd just entered the room, standing slowly to show a cordial respect. Grayson followed Rachel's lead.

The woman nodded. "Oh please, do sit down. We won't be long. Jack was gracious enough to allow me a few pre-meeting minutes with you…uh, Ms. Wheaton is it?"

"Yes, but you may call me Patricia."

"Yes, I see. Patricia. That's a very nice name," the woman said, her voice trailing off as she pulled a chair out from the table and sat down. "And you're Mr.-"

"Raphael. Michael Raphael," Grayson said, barely polite as he sat down. "We've met several times before." The air in the room stalled, suddenly stagnant.

"Good grief, is it getting stuffy in here?" Trader asked, chuckling as he stood up to find the thermostat. "This building is like one huge AI organism. The temp in here should be perfect."

"Maybe it's just you, darling," said the woman.

Trader winced.

*Interesting. Is he afraid of her?* Rachel sensed a kind of chaos between them. Priestly clearly had the upper hand. Had she humiliated Trader? Rachel thought so. Maybe more than once.

"Mrs. Priestly, is it?" Rachel asked as she took her chair. The woman nodded. "I'm sorry. I don't want to be rude, but have we met before?" Rachel smiled and looked directly at her, waiting for an answer.

"Gee darling, I don't think so," the woman said, her eyes narrowing as she tilted her head forward. "Do you?"

"Oh, it's probably nothing. It must have been someone who looks like you. It's not very often one sees such an impeccably dressed woman. Is that Versace?" Rachel asked.

"Why, yes it is, Ms. Wheaton. You have a good eye," Mrs. Priestly said.

"Yes. So I'm often told," Rachel said. The two women sized one another up, setting the rules of engagement for the meeting. The men had no idea what was going on.

"Lovely key," Rachel remarked. It was a good thing she'd secured the key case at the hotel. This time in a different place.

Mrs. Priestly smiled wryly. "Oh this? It's nothing, really. Just something I found hidden away in the back of a closet."

"Your closet I presume?" Rachel asked.

Mrs. Priestly ignored Rachel's repartee, and turned to

Trader. "Jack darling, let's get started. The others will be here soon."

Trader sat up straight. "Yes, of course." Opening the portfolio in front of him, he hesitated.

Grayson cleared his throat. "Hey, Jack. I appreciate you including me in this pre-interview session. Ms. Wheaton tells me she spent considerable time last evening researching *Virtual Life's* short history, particularly in the area of acquisitions. Might I suggest we spend some time talking about the overarching goal that drove those acquisitions?"

Trader looked over at Priestly for direction. All doubt about who was in charge had been removed.

"Yes, darling, let's do that," Mrs. Priestly said.

A chill ran down Rachel's back. Trader nodded tentatively. After a few seconds, he said, "No, I think not. First, that discussion will take much more time than we have, and second, we haven't yet made a formal offer to Ms. Wheaton. And...uh...there's no NDA in place."

Rachel could almost see the steam spewing from Mrs. Priestly's ears. Trader seemed to realize he'd stepped in it.

"However, I'm willing to attempt something this afternoon. The offer and the NDA, if it's still needed by then, can be taken care of by the end of the day. That said, I propose we schedule a subsequent meeting for the afternoon. We can brief Ms. Wheaton on the details of the mission then," Trader offered, recovering pretty well. Priestly sat back, apparently satisfied with his answer.

Rachel thought the acquisitions discussion, if it were to happen now, would be poorly timed. When she was on assignment, it was her practice to have an answer for every question that might arise, and a response to every scenario that might unfold. She knew quite a bit about the acquisitions already, but she wanted more time to prepare…more time to focus and connect the dots.

"Mrs. Priestly, I suggest we cover your agenda items," Trader said. "We have ten minutes before the others arrive."

Grayson looked poised to jump out of his chair. He was conspicuously tense around Mrs. Priestly, as if itching for any sign of provocation. Priestly abruptly swiveled her chair around, stood, and walked back toward the media curtain. Trader gave up his head-table seat and moved about six chairs away, presumably to give her a wider berth. Rachel sensed she was preparing to mark her territory. Her mind flashed on an image of the woman pacing the room as she made her proclamations, underscoring each with a dramatic gesture: standard fare for demonstrating dominance in a corporate hierarchy.

Priestly turned toward the window, unbuttoned her suit jacket and slipped it onto the back of Trader's former chair. She hovered over the table, putting both hands down spread wide on the surface while tilting her head ever so slightly, her eyes burrowing into each of the other three.

*She looks like a vulture ready to swoop.*

"Ah…such a lovely table. Have you talked with the designer yet about these chairs, Jack?" Trader gave her a blank look. "Uh huh, I see. Well, that's for another time. Now, what should we talk about first? Yes…Patricia…I want you to know that I'm here for you. If you have any questions, ideas, or suggestions, you just come to me and I'll make sure you get what you need. That's number one. Number two is this: As I'm sure you've learned through your research, *Virtual Life* has made extraordinary strides during the last 18 months. We'd like to see this trend continue. In order to ensure that happens, we'll need to be more aggressive in our market positioning."

Trader looked lame, hanging on Priestly's every word. Rachel had seen enough to know she was only using him as a pawn in her quest. She just didn't know specifically how or where Priestly intended to take them.

## Chapter Two

# THE AIM

The noisy hum of people talking outside the conference room doors grew louder. And then the double doors abruptly opened as the clock struck the hour. The executives entered slowly, talking quietly in pairs, walking huddled together as if into a memorial service. Silence settled like a blanket over the room while each person chose a seat. Mrs. Priestly remained standing at the head of the table until the doors closed and then moved to a chair two seats to the left, returning the one at the table's head to Trader.

Trader welcomed the congregants with a grandiose waving gesture, a rather awkward one at that. "Good morning, everyone. Coffee should be here momentarily," he said, smiling too broadly.

Rachel was distracted. Her spirit felt heavy, overwhelmed by a feeling of sadness so tragic, she could be at risk of performing poorly during the interview. She needed to shake it off, and quickly. The heaviness wasn't from her. It was in the room. She looked across the table, quickly and discretely glancing at each face. Nothing. Until she reached Grayson.

Grayson's face looked different: fallen. And his eyes were drooping. It dawned on her that during the few moments Mrs. Priestly had had the floor, Grayson's countenance turned uncharacteristically angry and annoyed. But it was more than angry and annoyed. Rachel realized that Grayson was grieving. Over what? Or who?

"Let's get started. We have a brief agenda today. Ms. Wheaton, yesterday afternoon we took the liberty of conducting what we call a pre-meeting, the purpose of which was to air any concerns or questions that might stall the progress of the interview. I feel confident that everyone is on board with our plan for today's second interview….unless anyone has any new concerns they'd like to raise?"

Trader looked around the table. Mrs. Priestly sat like a queen holding court, arrogance oozing from the tilt of her head to the way she sat cross-legged and indifferent in her expensive suit. She kept looking at Grayson, staring at him, communicating something secret and disturbing. Rachel tried to be discrete as she observed. The intensity of their dynamic seemed almost too obvious. Others would certainly notice unless Grayson pulled his emotions back and composed himself. She needed to do something, but wasn't certain if the enhanced sound system had been switched on. The notepad would work. She grabbed it from her bag and scribbled a brief message.

*Mr. Raphael, Thank you for walking alongside me through this process. It means more than you know.*

She leaned toward Grayson, sliding the note under his hand. He took it below the table surface to read, a faint smile relieving the tightness of his jaw. He whispered, "You're welcome. The pleasure is all mine."

She felt her face get warm and a slight thrill rise up into her chest. Maybe that was too much, but at least he would be okay for now. She wasn't so sure about herself. The fact that someone in the room could be linked to her parents' murder was no small distraction. If she let herself ponder the possibilities, the emotion would pull her down, rendering her useless for anyone, including *Virtual Life*. She had to get inside. Blowing her interview was not an option.

"All right...last call for concerns." Silence. "Okay, then. Let's get started. I'll cut right to the chase. Ms. Wheaton, we're prepared to make you an offer. The job itself will likely evolve in its form, but we all agree on the overarching purpose: to take the number 1 spot in the market."

It was a stunning proclamation. How did they expect her to do that?

Mrs. Priestly cleared her throat. "You look a little surprised. Don't tell me you're not aware of your own stellar reputation, Patricia. May I call you 'Patricia'?"

"Mrs. Priestly, I'm flattered, believe me. And I appreciate the confidence you all seem to have in my abilities. But I'm just a technologist, not a miracle worker. Were I to bring experience in market strategy and positioning, or technology innovations for that matter, it might be different. But honestly, I don't really see what *Virtual Life* sees in me."

"Oh, my dear Patricia, please don't be coy. We don't have time for that. There's work to do, and despite your own short-sightedness, you do have what we need to carry out our plans," Mrs. Priestly snarled through a stiff smile.

"You're much too flattering." Rachel paused, pretending to consider Mrs. Priestly's point. "Well, I suppose I might consider an offer, but I'd like to know more about this overarching purpose of yours. Mr. Trader described it as taking the number 1 spot in the market. How exactly do you plan on doing that? I mean really, unless you're planning on acquiring the top three companies, I don't see how you could possibly build the infrastructure necessary to eclipse your competitors."

A few of the executives looked down at the table, frantically scribbling notes. Rachel recognized the dodging tactic. Others sat up in their chairs, looking at her, and then Trader, and then back at her.

Trader perked up, as if a light bulb had switched on. "Service, Ms. Wheaton. Impeccable service. We plan on outdoing our competitors in social media up time and world-class customer support. You may have read that our competitors are already struggling to meet uptime demands. Their customers aren't going to put up with that very long, so we see this as a huge opportunity."

"So, your intent is to put the top 3 out of business?" Rachel asked.

"Uh…no, of course not. We here at *Virtual Life* believe in free market forces. If we can outperform the other guys, we think their customers will begin migrating over to *Virtual Life*. After all, we plan on offering the entire spectrum of social media services, and more. It would be a complete one-stop-shop relationship," Trader said. He looked over at Mrs. Priestly who nodded in approval.

Rachel was intrigued by the direction the interview had taken. "I see. Sounds like some kind of social media utopia. So your theory is that if you're successful, any customer establishing a *Virtual Life* account wouldn't want to go anywhere else, right? They could establish their virtual presence, connect with other *Virtual Life* customers, get all of their news, handle their business marketing, and run their business operations apps all through *Virtual Life*?"

"Exactly. That's the strategy," Trader said.

"Interesting. *Virtual Life* would then control all content, the look and feel of the interface, and the data security protocols across all social media experiences for what would be an increasingly larger base of customers. That seems…oh, how should I say it? Ambitious."

"Well, we like to think big around here, don't we?" Trader asked, looking around the table for agreement. The response was tepid at best, but no one disagreed. Mrs. Priestly looked like a tabby cat purring with delight at the end of the table.

Rachel decided to back off the harder questions for the time being and make a hard-left shift to next steps. "It all sounds quite intriguing. But I need to know a few things before I'm willing to entertain an offer. Most importantly, I want to know what success looks like in your minds. Aspects such as performance indicators, timeframes, support resources at my disposal, etc. I cannot, in good conscience, blindly accept a job offer based only upon a flattering assessment of my value," Rachel said, noticing Grayson had turned completely round in his chair to face her as she spoke. So had several others at the table.

Mrs. Priestly chimed in. "I see. I suppose that's a fair expectation. Jack, have a modified offer letter drawn up with acceptance contingent upon agreement on a job performance plan for Ms. Wheaton."

Trader coughed. "Thank you for your suggestion, Veronica. Let's see…let me give this a think." Trader looked up and down the table, presumably to seek input from the others. No takers…again. He continued. "Ms. Wheaton, in my few years as CEO, I've learned better than most how important it is to build a good team. I appreciate your concern and agree that it's only fair to allow you some insight into my starting list of team members. I've asked Calista Lawrence, head of Systems Improvement and Innovation, and George Kendall over Market Research and Media Innovation to select their top people and devote them to your team on a full-time basis."

Rachel saw an opportunity. "That sounds workable, but I have one request. I've learned through my acquisitions research that Mr. Haddad probably works for Ms. Lawrence. I'd like to request that he be considered for the team."

Trader looked surprised. "Ms. Wheaton, as you can see, Syed is not in attendance today. He's still in re…uh, enjoying some family time at home. I'm not sure he's the best choice, at least not under the circumstances."

"And what circumstances would those be?" Rachel asked.

"Excuse me," interrupted Ms. Lawrence. "Syed Haddad is under consideration for a transfer to a different group. Trust me, Ms. Wheaton; I am fully capable of selecting a suitable team member for your little endeavor. You just leave that to me-"

"Now Calista darling, there's no need to diminish the importance of Ms. Wheaton's potential role with the company," Mrs. Priestly said, obviously enjoying the exchange. Ms. Lawrence sat back, acquiescing to Mrs. Priestly.

"Ms. Wheaton, Syed may not be suitable for your team, but I would be happy to facilitate a discussion with just the three of us at your convenience. Say…next week, assuming Mr. Haddad returns to work," Mrs. Priestly said.

"That's very generous of you, Mrs. Priestly, but if there's going to be a discussion with Mr. Haddad, I'd prefer to set the conditions," Rachel said.

Grayson turned toward the group. "Jack, if you'd like, I can continue in the role I've been playing in regard to Ms. Wheaton's recruitment process. I'd be happy to facilitate any discussions she might want to have with specific team members. That is, if she's comfortable with my presence," Grayson said.

"Oh, no you-," Mrs. Priestly started.

"Veronica, let me handle this," Trader said. "Michael, I think that's a good compromise. I'm fine with you continuing in that role. In fact, consider yourself the point person for coordinating any additional discussions."

Mrs. Priestly shot Grayson some real daggers, but he didn't respond in kind. Rachel thought it was weird...he actually smiled at her. Not a sarcastic smile. It looked more like pity mixed with a pinch of triumph.

"Thanks Jack. Now that we've gotten that out of the way, do you want to talk offer?" Grayson asked.

"Yes, of course," Trader said. "Ms. Wheaton, we're prepared to offer you an annual salary of $625,000 plus a bonus of up to 150% of your base pay contingent upon achievement of performance targets. We'd like you to start as soon as possible pending agreement on a performance plan and selection of the specific members of your team."

Rachel couldn't believe her ears. $625,000 was an awful lot of money for a technologist. *Virtual Life* obviously wanted her for more than her data forensics skills. Just gaining possession of the key case couldn't possibly account for such a grandiose offer. There was something else.

"That's a very generous offer, Mr. Trader," Rachel said, trying not to show her surprise. "I'll take it under advisement. In the meantime, I'd like to begin working with Mr. Raphael. We can start by creating a team profile from which to develop a list of proposed candidates. If we start right away, we can have a list by tomorrow afternoon," Rachel said.

There was an interesting stir in the room, as if the group was unaccustomed to a person asserting their wishes. Trader sat up a little taller, seemingly satisfied with how Rachel had effectively ignored Mrs. Priestly during the discussion.

"Yes, Ms. Wheaton. That sounds fine," Trader said, glancing smugly at Mrs. Priestly. The look on her face promised trouble later on.

"Great. Then Mr. Raphael and I will be off to start talking profiles," Rachel said, standing to leave. Several of the others rose as well, quiet but nodding in agreement. "We will be in contact," Grayson said as he followed Rachel out of the room.

The elevator door closed behind them. Rachel gave Grayson a questioning glance. She wondered what was going on between him and Mrs. Priestly.

Grayson shook his head as if he knew what was on her mind. He looked exhausted.

*Chapter Three*

# TEA TIME

The ride back to The Kimberly passed with only the sound of *Diana Krall* singing softly through the back passenger sound system. Grayson didn't seem like his usual upbeat self. Rachel thought it better not to push. The truth would emerge on its own and in its own time.

They decided to meet later at Grayson's "Michael Raphael" loft in Tribeca to start working on a plan. And then dinner. In the meantime, Rachel wanted to steal away for a few quiet hours.

"We're here. Here's the address of my loft. How about we get an early start, say around 3 o'clock?" Grayson asked as he handed her the slip of paper. The limo slowly came to a stop before the passenger door was opened by one of the hotel doormen.

"That sounds perfect," Rachel said. She studied Grayson's face, trying to gauge his feelings. "Are you all right?"

"No, not really." He paused, realizing Rachel might be

thinking it was something she'd said or done. "No no...it has nothing to do with you. And I don't want you to think it does, you understand me?" A hint of a smile broke around his eyes and the corners of his mouth. "Things are difficult for me right now." He paused. "Um...I'm not at liberty-"

"Gray...Michael, if there's anything I can do to help, please let me know. Don't hesitate. Please."

"Ms. Wheaton, you've already helped me more than you know."

Rachel smiled, shook Grayson's hand, and said, "Thank you, Mr. Raphael. I will see you at 3 o'clock." Grayson nodded his goodbye and the waiting doorman's white gloved hand took hers, assisting her out of the limo's passenger cab. It was Charles Bannister, at her service.

"Good afternoon, Ms. Wheaton. How are you today?" Charles asked.

"I'm doing well, Charles. Thank you for asking. The more important question is 'how are you doing?'"

"I'm well, Ms. Wheaton. I see you're still getting the star treatment," Charles said as the two of them watched the limo drive away. Grayson saluted her through the back window as the vehicle disappeared down the street.

"Yes, he's a very nice man," Rachel said, letting a little dreamy-eyed sigh accidentally escape.

Charles smiled.

"What?" Rachel stammered.

"Oh, nothing. Nothing at all, Ms. Wheaton." Charles cleared his throat. "However, I do have a message for you. Amir, the concierge, would like you to stop by his podium at your earliest convenience. He will be on duty until 6 o'clock tonight. I think he has set up something special for you in your room. Don't tell him I told you. He might want it to be a surprise."

"Well, I can see I need to be careful with what I tell you in the future!" Rachel said, chuckling.

"Yes, I suppose you're correct. Have a good afternoon, Ms. Wheaton."

"Thanks Charles. You too," Rachel said as she turned toward the hotel entrance.

*A request from Amir - that means something's up.*

A few dozen people milled around the hotel foyer, most of them congregating near the registrar's desk. And something new: a string quartet situated at the end of the long dark hallway playing a beautiful piece by Tchaikovsky. The group's moody strings filled the atmosphere with a sweet romantic ambiance that took Rachel into a soul-dreamy state. One of the violinists caught her eye and smiled, nodding once to acknowledge her appreciation of the music.

A middle-aged couple stood at the concierge podium, talking with Amir about restaurants and theatre tickets. He held his reliable clipboard, flipping through the latest theatre flyers to sort out ticket options for his guests. Rachel waited in line a few feet behind the couple, catching Amir's eye. He grinned, seemingly glad to see her.

"You're all set, Mr. and Mrs. Knight," Amir said as he handed them their dinner reservation details and theatre tickets. Rachel stepped up as they departed.

"Good day, Ms. Wheaton. It's wonderful to see you," Amir said. "How was your interview this morning?"

"It was interesting, to be sure. Very intriguing. They have some big ideas; maybe too big. Uh…anyway, Charles asked me to check in with you. Do you have time to talk now?"

Amir looked up, noting the line forming behind Rachel. "I'm scheduled for a break in 20 minutes. Is it possible for you to wait until then? We could talk over a cup of tea if you'd like."

"I would love to. Where would you like to meet?" Rachel asked.

"There's a tea house two doors down. It's called *Radiance Tea House and Books*. I can meet you there at 10:35."

"That's perfect. That gives me time to change. I'm looking forward to it," Rachel said as she stepped aside to make room for the next guest. Amir nodded his agreement and gave her a friendly salute before turning to the next in line. "Good morning sir. How may I help you today?"

Rachel grabbed the first empty elevator car and made it to her room in record time. The room had been made up, this time in no extraordinary way. She hadn't yet finished her review of the entry logs Amir had gathered for her. With *Dennis* out of the picture, it didn't seem like a high priority. Or so she told herself. She had to admit, it bothered her, and she wasn't one to let nagging thoughts linger too long. She knew she'd push herself to make the time, but this was a tough one.

The idea of someone going through all of her personal things without her permission brought back a wave of hurt from the past. Some of the foster families she'd lived with were paranoid suspicious types, always putting her under watch; searching her room; and scrutinizing everything she said or did. They constantly questioned her motives and character. It was demoralizing. She wasn't sure she'd ever really recovered from the trauma.

Through those years, the entire time, Rachel always knew deep inside that she wasn't alone. There had been a presence. It guided her, often steering her down unexpected paths: better and safer paths. Her parents openly talked about the presence of a Guide in their lives. Both her mother and father were temperamentally humble and sweet, often feeling just as much in awe of their own innovative ideas as anyone else. Her mother once said that she and her father often found themselves working within a creative zone, plucking ideas from the air as the two engaged in brain storming sessions, feeding off the energy thrown up by the ideas themselves. The harmony and synergy of the ideas fell into place with no effort on their part. Her mom believed the ideas were there for them to discover.

Time was precious, especially today. Rachel shook off her train of thought and started toward the bedroom.

"*Gasp*! Oh my gosh…this is awesome!"

There, halfway down the hallway sitting on a narrow console, was a phone-charging dock that doubled as a sound system. A very nice sound system, at that.

"Oh my gosh, this is so sweet."

She was touched. Her eyes welled up, and her chin quivered. On the rare occasion when someone unexpectedly did something for her, she felt overwhelmed. Like she'd been seen. And understood. There was nothing else like it.

She grabbed her phone and chose a jazz station, set it on the dock, and turned on the sound. A rich and soulful melody instantly filled the suite. Although it would have been fun to hang out for a bit, it was time to get moving. Fed up with fitted suits and heels, she grabbed a pair of Fabrizio Giani cigarette pants from the closet, pairing them with a tailored cotton blouse and some comfortable flats. The pants weren't the most flattering, showing slightly too much definition of her muscular legs, but they were the most comfortable. Despite the fun of sporting designer suits and killer shoes, it was time to go incognito and blend in. Checking herself in the mirror one more time, she switched off the music, grabbed her phone off the dock, and headed to the lobby.

The fresher than usual morning air gave her a shot of energy as she exited the hotel and took a left down E. 50th, walking quickly toward the restaurant located mid-block between 3rd and 2nd. If it were this same hour on a day moving toward summer, the air would not be as sweet and refreshing. Fortunately for her and her hair, the humidity hadn't yet arrived. She held no nostalgia for the smell of garbage in the too-moist air of the summer streets. Sanitation worker strikes were not unheard of; the city could be due for another.

The wind came up, sending an untimely breath of warmth right through to her insides, a breath instilling within her a peaceful readiness. Any weariness or frazzled nerves had suddenly become memories. These "out of nowhere" winds of change usually happened when she least expected it, which made the experience all the more powerful in its affect. Sometimes there wasn't a wind; only a stirring of energy in her chest like when her dad would drive the jeep too fast over the hills on her Aunt's farm, catching air over every rise. It was a thrilling feeling, emboldening her to run directly toward the next great challenge.

Renewed in spirit, Rachel quickened her gait, reaching the entry doors of *Radiance Tea House and Books* at 10:35 am.

## Chapter Four

# VAGUE RECOLLECTIONS

A mir followed her in.

"Oh! Why didn't you say something? Were you right behind me?" Rachel asked.

"Yes, but I can't keep up with you!"

"What's the matter, Amir? A little out of shape, are you?" Rachel asked. He looked deflated. "Oh come on, I'm just kidding."

"Hah…yes, I suppose you're right, Ms. Wheaton. I do feel at ease with you. Let's get a table and order. I've reserved one of the booths," Amir said.

"Okie dokie. Let's do this!" Rachel said. She felt almost giddy with anticipation about her "adventure." The tea house host, who obviously knew Amir, exchanged a few whispers with Amir before escorting them to a table away from the main seating area.

"Amir, did you want to tell me something about my room?" Rachel asked, a twinkle in her eye.

"I'm sorry, Ms. Wheaton, I'm not sure I understand what you're talking about," Amir said.

"Come on, Amir. I know what you did. And it was absolutely lovely and fabulous and thoughtful! It made me cry... a little. How did you know-,"

"Ms. Wheaton, you're very welcome," Amir said, smiling warmly. "But I can't take all the credit for it."

"What do you mean?" Rachel didn't like surprises. At least not the kind that meant trouble.

Amir stopped, realizing she was concerned. "Oh no, its fine, really. I happened to mention to the gentleman who's been accompanying you in your various limousine rides that-"

"You mean Mr. Raphael?" Rachel asked.

"Yes, I believe that's his name. Anyway, he overheard me mention that we received a comment from a guest regarding the music coming from your room yesterday morning. He asked if I knew who the artist was and as it happened, the guest who had complained...er...I mean commented about the noise mentioned the group. I've never heard of them. It was something like *Slinky and the Family*. Mr. Raphael knew right away who it was. Anyway, that's what happened. He arranged for me to setup a sound system so that you might find listening more enjoyable. I assumed it would be all right since the two of you seemed friendly. At least that's what Charles said."

Rachel was relieved. "Charles, huh? I'll have to have a little chat with him," Rachel said, smiling. "So wow...that's really something. I mean, really, that's something, Amir. Mr. Raphael seems like a considerate person, don't you think? I think so. And you...well, you're an incredible concierge," Rachel said.

A smartly uniformed server appeared at table-side to take their order. "Good morning, sir. Would you like your usual selection today?"

Amir looked at Rachel, considering what she might prefer. "Yes, I think that will be best," Amir said. "Thank you, Jai."

"As you wish, sir." Jai disappeared to go take care of the order.

Amir looked down, quiet. He seemed to be searching for words. She waited, watching, reading his demeanor.

"It's okay, Amir. Take your time."

Amir looked up. His expression was familiar, like another deja vu. Not two hours before Grayson's face had looked the same.

"What's wrong, Amir? Why are you sad?"

"Ms. Wheaton, I'm sorry, but this isn't easy. It won't be easy for you either."

Rachel wasn't sure where Amir was going, but didn't want him to pull back. "Please, go on," Rachel said.

"Okay." Amir took another deep breath. "I have a dear friend. We've been friends since university, closer than brothers, and I know if the tables were turned, he would want to do all he could for me." He sighed. "Ms. Wheaton. He's in serious trouble. And I need your help."

"My help? Gee…I wasn't expecting that. Um…okay…yes, of course. If I can help, I certainly will. Go on."

"My friend and I have always been there for each other, but I think we're facing a difficult challenge." Amir's eyes turned glassy. "Ms. Wheaton, someone is putting pressure on him, forcing him to do things he doesn't want to do. They're threatening to hurt his family, including his sister, my fiancé."

*Bloody hell.*

"I'm a little confused. Does this have something to do with me? Why do you think I can help him?"

"The people threatening him are affiliated with *Virtual Life*."

*What? Could it…*

"Amir…what's your friend's name?"

"Syed Haddad."

*Why did I know that?*

The server appeared with a tray of tea selections, including two beautiful teacups trimmed in 14K gold, vibrant with colorful designs hand painted on the polished porcelain surface. They were distractingly beautiful, catching Rachel's eye.

"Pardon me, madam. Is there anything else I can bring you?" Jai asked.

"Oh no, thank you. This is wonderful," Rachel said. He nodded toward Amir and disappeared to the front of the tea room.

Amir poured hot water into each of the cups, intermittently sneaking a peek at Rachel, waiting for her response. "I recommend this special blend. It's both soothing to the throat and pleasant on the palate. May I?" Amir asked before putting the infuser into her cup.

"Yes, that's perfect. Thank you." Rachel's head swirled with memories, impressions, and fuzzy images. She was missing something. And then a question

"Amir, do you know me?" Rachel asked.

"Yes, you're Ms. Wheaton," Amir said.

"No, that's not what I mean. I'm asking if you know me. If you know me from before," Rachel said.

His face changed, resigning to the inevitable.

Amir sighed. "Yes, Rachel."

Rachel trembled, her skin tingling. "I remember the first morning I talked with you at The Kimberly. You called me by my name. A slip of the tongue?"

"That was a mistake, but I was overwhelmed at seeing you again. You were such a smart and vibrant girl, so sensitive and intuitive. Just like your parents."

Rachel's heart began racing.

"I was there, in Jerusalem. Syed was there, working with your parents. We were friends, all of us."

Rachel's memories tried to push their way into her thoughts, but she'd repressed them so long, she'd forgotten how to let them in. Since her arrival at The Kimberly, she'd felt there was something familiar about him. But now the emotions came rushing in. She and Amir had some sort of timeless bond. Just looking at him told her that. His eyes held the knowledge of a young girl's devastating loss; a loss that he'd suffered too. It was the kind of bond forged in a moment that could never be erased despite the passing of so many decades since.

"I grew quite fond of your family. And you…well, you were special. I'm so sorry…"

"You know, I knew it. I mean, I didn't really know it in my head, but I knew it in my gut."

"I knew you recognized me, but you didn't seem to remember from where. It was a long time ago."

Rachel didn't know what to say. It was all so personal, but she had a job to do. How was she going to get through this with a clear head?

"Amir, how are you here? Now? Why are you here?"

"Rachel, I don't have all the answers. All I know is that some really strange coincidences occurred to get me here. It almost felt like divine intervention. There's really no other explanation for it. I left the Middle East years ago, but Syed and I stayed in contact. For several months I heard nothing. I was living in Salisbury at the time when Syed's wife called me one night, frantic. He'd gone missing the day before. She was afraid and asked for my help. I've been trying to find and bring him home ever since."

"Two years? You've been looking for him for two years?" Rachel asked, trying to put the timelines together in her mind. The information she'd gathered from the acquisitions research fit with what Amir was telling her. It's possible Syed was pulled into the pre-acquisition effort. Maybe against his will?

"Yes. I was brought here by a 'Mr. Randal.' I've not met him in person yet, but I feel like he's always near by."

"What do you mean, 'near by?'"

"I'm not sure. It's as if he's not quite here but then he's always here. I don't know what I'm saying. It's just that, well...the way things go...I don't know how to describe it. It's beyond coincidence. Anyway, I know Syed is here in New York, working for the company you're interviewing with. I'm hoping you'll connect with him," Amir said.

Amir lifted the tea to his mouth for a sip. Rachel noticed a tremble in his hand. His face was flushed.

"Amir, I wouldn't say no to you. Of course, I will help," Rachel said. Already her wheels were spinning, sorting what Syed's presence might mean going forward. "I have something to tell you. I probably shouldn't, but it seems to be the next thing."

Amir leaned forward, listening. Rachel began. "I've done some research on the business activities conducted by *Virtual Life* over the last 18 months. There was an acquisition of a company based in Jerusalem. It happened around the same time you say your friend Syed disappeared. I suspect the company was either owned by Syed or he played a prominent role in its operations. So far, I haven't been allowed to ask any specific questions of individual executives, but that all changed today. If I accept the job offer with *Virtual Life*, I'll need a team. Today I received approval from the CEO to interview internal candidates for the team...and I requested that Syed Haddad be put on the list."

"Oh my, Ms. Wheaton...Rachel. That's wonderful-," Amir started.

"But wait. There's a problem. Syed had an episode yesterday during the first interview."

"What do you mean 'an episode'?"

"At one point I was given the floor to ask a question about the acquisitions. I'd barely gotten my first question out and Syed became agitated and started perspiring. He had to take his jacket off. Then he started having trouble breathing. I know because *Virtual Life* has this crazy sound system that picks up every breath, whisper, or word uttered within the space, amplifying it over some kind of PA system. It was weird. I watched him, expecting someone to come to his assistance, but no one else paid any attention. I eventually had to say something, and when I did, Syed was forcibly escorted out of the room. The whole incident really shook me."

"Oh my gosh." Amir looked worried. "Syed has had respiratory and autoimmune system issues since his late twenties. Maybe he's ill," Amir said.

"Maybe so. Today when I asked that he be included on the list of interviewees, I was told he's still unavailable and that he's being considered for a transfer of some type. It felt like a phony story to keep me from gaining access to him."

"We need to find him, and soon," Amir said. "The last time I talked…"

"Amir, I'm banking on Mr. Trader's commitment to allow Syed to interview for a team member role. If Trader keeps his word, I'll be seeing Syed very soon."

Rachel realized she'd cut him off, but he was too polite to interrupt her. "I'm sorry. You wanted to say something. Tell me more. You've talked with him?" Rachel asked.

"Just two times. The first time he called, he wanted to tell me something, but before he could, another call came in on his line. He put me on hold and when he came back, he was different."

"Different?"

"Uh huh. Tentative. Afraid. He was very terse toward me, which isn't like him. I was taken aback by the change. I regret not having the presence of mind to question him. By the time I recovered, he'd already hung up," Amir said. He looked dejected. "If only I'd been quicker, I might have been able to find out where he was."

"But you talked with him a second time?"

"I did, but it was different. He called me again - it was from an unknown number - and I couldn't hear what he was saying. He was whispering. I heard people in the background...other voices...a woman's voice. And a man, but there seemed to be other noises too, like he was in some kind of common work area."

"Like a cubicle farm?" Rachel asked.

"A cubicle farm?"

"That's what I call it. It's usually a large room with rows of rectangular work spaces divided by partial walls. Each cubicle has a workstation and a chair, and not much else. Maybe a few overhead bins. There's really no way to have a private conversation. Visual privacy is minimal, especially when people walk the hall and look over the wall into your workspace. That means that even though there could be a hundred people packed into a small space, it's usually pretty quiet because they don't want their conversations to be overheard. The only other sound is from the keyboards clicking, chairs moving...those kinds of things. Did it sound like that kind of a space?"

Amir was staring at Rachel like she was speaking Martian. "Wow...I've never seen one, but I guess it could have been a 'cubicle farm.'"

"I'm guessing Syed called you from *Virtual Life*. During either of those calls, did he mention where he's living? And with whom?" Rachel asked.

"I asked him. It was on the first call. He wouldn't answer me. Something about not wanting me to know too much. It was unlike him. We've always been open with each other. My stomach churned as I listened to him, like my instincts were trying to tell me something was wrong. I wondered if he was lying, or playing a role. Does that sound strange?"

"No. That doesn't sound strange. I get the feeling that most of the people at *Virtual Life* are playing roles, whether they want to or not."

Amir looked lost. "Rachel, what do I do now?"

"I'm not sure, Amir. We'll need to wait and watch." Their eyes locked, now joined together in a common pursuit.

## Chapter Five

# A SIGHTING

Jai came back to the table. "Is there anything else I can bring you this morning?"

"No. Thank you, Jai. The tea was exquisite as usual," Amir said.

"As you wish," Jai said.

Rachel's ears perked up. *"As you wish"...there's that little phrase again.*

"I bet he's a good server. Seems experienced. Gosh, it feels like we've been here for hours. Don't you need to be back? What time is it anyway?" Rachel asked.

"Time? Let's see. Oh...I don't have a watch. That's weird. How could I forget that?" Amir looked past Rachel. "And I don't see a clock. Why don't you go ahead without me? I'll take care of the tab." Amir said. "I want to pick up some tea to take home anyway."

"Oh, all right. I'll be at the hotel until mid afternoon if

anything else comes up, okay? Don't hesitate to ring the room."

"Thank you, Rachel. I won't hesitate."

"Promise?"

"I promise. I'm so grateful…" Amir hung his head, trying to hold back the emotions.

"It's all right. I'll see you later. And…be careful," Rachel said.

"I will. You be careful too."

Amir headed toward the front counter while Rachel walked to the exit. She hoped she still had time to recharge before catching a cab for Tribeca. The walk back to The Kimberly would give her a chance to think. She was tempted to sort through the implications of what Amir had told her, but knew it would be more productive to take a break and give her brain a rest.

Rachel waited for an opening in the crowd before stepping out onto the cement sidewalk.

*Uhmph!*

Shoved by an oncoming shoulder, her body suddenly spun round and headed down. The next thing she saw was the cracked concrete sidewalk speeding upward towards her face. The reflexes kicked in, her hands hit the pavement, and she let herself down.

"Oh my goodness, Miss. I'm so sorry, I didn't see you!" It was a man's voice. Someone grabbed her upper arm and lifted her to her feet, but when she looked, there wasn't any one there, only a dense crowd; too dense to detect the person who shoved her. She froze and waited, watching, knowing that whoever it was, he would look back.

Suddenly, all went quiet, as if someone had turned the sound off. Pedestrians walked in slow motion, the women's hair bouncing up and down like in a Breck commercial, and the men's pant legs flowing back and forth with each step. The faces of the oncoming went gray. The backs of those walking away were now only shadows. And then up ahead, maybe 50 yards or so, a glow rose above the crowd. As Rachel followed the path of light with her eyes, the crowd parted to reveal a single man who'd paused to turn and look at her. The light was too much.

*Uh oh…*

Blinded, Rachel froze, wondering if she was having some kind of hallucination. Then her sight returned just as suddenly as she'd lost it. The man was still standing among the slow moving shadow people, the only source of light in the midst of the darkened crowd. He seemed staid. No smile. No nod. Rachel felt fear, but she wasn't afraid. It was a feeling of awe.

She thought she knew his face, but couldn't recall where she'd seen him before. Replaying the scenes of the past 48 hours, she searched the peripheries of the rooms she'd been in, people she'd noticed on the streets, and guests loitering in the hotel foyer. Nothing. Did the man run into her on purpose? She needed to know.

"Hey! Sir…hold up! Sir!" Rachel shouted, getting no response.

Time suddenly switched to a normal tick, the crowd converging once again and blocking her view. She thought to chase him down, but something stopped her, a momentary paralysis. Faces from the past few days streamed through her mind. And then…

*He was in the Virtual Life conference room. But…was he at the table? I don't see him at the table.*

Rachel moved out of the flow of foot traffic and stood under a storefront canopy, searching through the crowds up and down the street, trying to catch another glimpse of the man. By then the swarm of pedestrians had completely blocked her view. She noticed a clock in the storefront windows.

*11:00 am.*

"11:00? That's not possible," she whispered to herself. How could so little time have passed given the long tea break with Amir? Maybe their talk only felt like a long one because…well, she didn't know why. In any case, it was only 11:00 am. She had plenty of time to recharge before her trip to Tribeca. Maybe Grayson would be able to place the man.

Her legs were wobbly and her hands kept trembling. "Okay, I'm a little freaked out," she muttered under her breath.

A ferocious wind came up as she turned west on E. 50th, blowing a frigid gust right through her skin, and probably the skin of every pedestrian in her lane of traffic. She shivered uncontrollably, kicking herself for not grabbing the overcoat off the chair in her room. Or her pistol for that matter, although she didn't have the key case on her person. *Dennis* was out of the picture and the key was hidden away, secure for now.

Looking up to see how much further she had to walk, a wonderful sight came into view.

*I don't believe it. Is that Charles?*

"You've got to be kidding me!" Rachel said. "Are you guys clairvoyant, or what?"

Charles chuckled. "No, not at all, Ms. Wheaton. I noticed the temperature had dropped and thought you might need your coat. I hope you don't mind. I let myself into your room to retrieve it," Charles said.

"Are you kidding? I love how you guys take such great care of me. It's almost uncanny, isn't it?" Rachel slipped the coat on. "Ah. Much better. Let's go…it's cold out here!"

"Yes, ma'am," Charles said.

*Chapter Six*

# PORTALS

T he late morning sun streamed through the freshly cleaned windows, casting a warm light on the overstuffed chair. She grabbed her ebook reader for the first time since arriving in Manhattan, hoping to discover a sparkling word. Her perspective had taken a beating over the past 36 hours; too many memories pushing to rush in, dragging with them another voice accusing her of an inherent unworthiness. Beating them back left her exhausted.

Rachel sometimes wondered why her life had gone as it had. She never wanted her spirit to grow brittle, but the weight of grief she felt about losing her parents was wearing. She'd found a little solace in work: school and career becoming her drugs of choice. They were the only all-consuming "productive" distractions that kept her mind busy with the here and now while moving forward with her life. But that had only taken her so far.

There were still imbalanced days; days like the past two when the intensity of her assignment, the rush to beat time, and the need to bring order out of chaos eventually drained her, narrowing her perspective and blocking out the broader view. Her old mental patterns were gathering strength: the willfulness, the self-determination to prove her worth, and the intense need to drive things to a final resolution. She had noticed a weariness coming on. The best thing for her to do was to stop and be still, allowing herself to recharge and let the seemingly irrelevant re-enter the span of her attention.

Rachel closed her eyes, accepting the muffled sounds from the street below, comforted by the warmth radiating through the windows. The anxiety faded, bringing calm like a gentle wave that dissipates and ebbs onto an undisturbed beach.

Forty-five minutes later she opened her eyes to a new start. The first book in the e-reader would be fine.

There was a sparkle.

> *"...Something catches your attention—some Paul Simon tune, the way the sunlight moves on the floor lengthening the shadows, the earthy smell of espresso—and a trapdoor opens to the world that runs below the surface of your life. You fall through. Two seconds pass between that moment and when the barista starts snapping his fingers in your face, but you wake up a lifetime later. This sort of thing also happens in the deep doorways outside shops in Boston, in huge wooden wardrobes, in museum paintings and looking glasses—portals, all of them, to kairos."*[2]

"Elevators too."

The thunderous pounding on the door awakened Rachel from what had felt like an eternal second. There were only a few who knew she was there and even fewer who knew her room number. It couldn't be Grayson; he was at his apartment in Tribeca.

The clock said 12:45 pm. She was hungry. Could it be room

service? The two dapper fellows downstairs had done well when anticipating her needs before, so why not now? She tiptoed across the room, not wanting to make any noise that might give her away. The door's peep hole was placed below eye level, a good thing. She might be able to get a look without notice.

A brilliant red filled the fish-eyed glass, someone's suit jacket in a shade too bright for a bellhop. Stepping back slow and silent, she turned toward the bedroom. Four more demanding knocks rang out. A hotel staff person wouldn't do that. The house phone sat on the nightstand just inside the bedroom. Rachel pressed the "Concierge" button and waited, hoping Amir would pick up.

"Yes, Ms. Wheaton, how may I assist you?" Amir answered.

"Amir, it's me," Rachel whispered.

"Yes, I know. Is there a problem?" Amir asked.

"I don't know. There's someone pounding on the door. I can't tell who it is, but they're wearing a bright red suit."

"Could it be staff? Possibly one of the bellmen…or a doorman?"

"No, I don't think so. The color's too bright. It looks like the kind of red a woman would wear. Would you please see if security…or better yet, would you see if Charles can come up to investigate?"

"Certainly, right away."

Rachel gently placed the receiver in the cradle and tiptoed back to the living area. The pounding had morphed into a rapid knocking. Looking through the peep hole again, she could see she was right: it was a woman in red. She still couldn't see the face. It would make too much noise to try and hunch down on the floor for a better look; too risky.

Standing still and quiet, like a statue, she waited for Charles.

*Friend or foe? I'm guessing "foe."*

The sound of heavy footsteps announced the possible arrival of assistance. She heard a man's muffled voice. More footsteps.

"Pardon me?" a woman said.

"I said good afternoon, ma'am. May I assist you with something?" It was Charles. Charles Bannister. Rachel breathed a sigh of relief. The last thing she wanted was to be caught and cornered by an unknown.

"Uh yes, I think I might be lost. I'm looking for my daughter's room. I'm certain she told me it was this room number, but no one seems to be here," said the woman.

"I see, Ms.?" Charles said.

"Uh, Wheaton. Mrs. Wheaton."

"Yes, I see Mrs. Wheaton. I'm happy to escort you to the registrar where they can help you make contact with your daughter," Charles said. Rachel listened, entertained by the load of baloney being dished out. She took another look through the peep hole.

*What? Calista Lawrence? What does she want?*

"Oh, I don't want to be a bother. I'll just wait here until she gets back," the woman said.

"I'm sorry, Ma'am, but access to the hotel's room accommodations is restricted to registered guests only. Please come with me," Charles said.

"Well, don't you have a key? Can't you just let me into the room so that I can be out of the way while I wait for her?" the woman asked.

"Ma'am, if you don't come with me right now, I'll be forced to call security and have you removed from the premises," Charles said.

*That's my Charles. No nonsense.*

"Well, you can't blame a girl for trying now, can you?"

*Oh brother…taking lessons from Priestly.*

"No Ma'am. I'm happy to escort you out of the hotel and into the next cab. Please, after you," Charles said, directing the woman away from the door and down the hall to the elevators.

She watched them move out of sight before phoning Amir.

"Yes, Ms. Wheaton. Was everything carried out to your satisfaction?" Amir asked.

"Yes. Perfectly. So, Amir…this may seem a little off topic, but I'm famished. Would you mind having some lunch sent up? I have about 90 minutes before I need to catch a cab for Tribeca."

"As you wish. I'll take care of it right away."

"Thank you. You're a gem. Oh…and Amir…I don't want to ask too much of you, but would it be possible to arrange for a room transfer? I'm afraid my room number has been compromised."

"Yes, of course. I'll arrange for another room right now. When would you like to make the switch?"

"Let's do the switch right before I leave, around ten after 2. Um…let's see if there's anything else. I'm sorry. I know I'm high maintenance.

"Ms. Wheaton, if you don't mind me saying so, you're anything but high maintenance. Whatever you need, I'm at your service," Amir said.

"You're so good. Just one more thing. I need access to a secure safe. The most secure safe available."

"No problem, Ms. Wheaton."

"Bless you, Amir. I'll let you know when I'm ready. Shouldn't be too long."

Rachel hung up and sat down in the overstuffed chair. Calista had trampled her calm silence with her incessant knocking. She needed a few minutes to re-center, but it was time for work. Rachel took a chair at the table and began reviewing the pile of information she'd accumulated over the past 36 hours. The list of entries into her room, the acquisitions G2, and the latest data transmission readouts.

*A smart woman's thinking is never done.*

[2]*Praying the Hours in Ordinary Life: (Art for Faith's Sake)*
*Lauralee Farrer and Clayton J. Schmit*

## Chapter Seven

# DOTS

R achel took the last bite of a delicious salmon over greens salad. A little nourishment always made her feel better. The Chai tea hadn't hurt either. She was ready to dive into a big pile of what promised to be tedious analytical work.

The images had been brewing in the back of her mind for the past day. Intruders entering her room while she was away, masking their true purpose with a world-class cleaning job. The report from Amir might offer up some clues. Who had "cleaned" the room? Who had slipped in to deliver the Armani suit? And given the afternoon's unexpected visitor, how did Calista Lawrence know her room number?

*Heck, why don't they just all come by? We can have a party...get to know each other.*

The format was simple: entry and exit times matched with a keycard ID number. After accounting for her own activity, there were two log items left. The first showed one access with a time stamp of 11:20 am. It looked like a single "open door" item, indicating someone opened the door, held it open, and then left before it closed. Rachel was in the bedroom at the time, having just returned from Zabars. She hadn't heard anything. Someone could have quietly opened the door, hung the Armani on the inside hook, and left, closing the door behind them. Oddly, the key card ID field was blank. Could she have left the door ajar and not realized it? If she did, the delivery person wouldn't need a card to get in. But then how was the moment of access captured on the report? She didn't know their system, but Amir might. Or he knows a guy who knows.

The next access occurred at 1:15 pm. Someone, or some number of people, entered the room and remained there for over an hour, exiting at 2:20 pm. She had returned from the *Virtual Life* interview between 2:30 and 3:00 pm. The room looked fantastic. Her clothes had been carefully hung in the closet, and her personal toiletry and beauty products had been placed neatly on the floating shelves and in the cupboards of the en suite. But even with the extra time it must have taken to do the super cleaning, it wouldn't have taken over an hour. Obviously, whoever it was, spent a good part of the time doing something else…like looking for the key case. This time, the report included a keycard ID, which meant she could probably track down who had done the dirty deed.

*Make that "the clean deed."*

Rachel jotted her usual cryptic notes directly on the report and put it back into the concealed compartment of her garment bag. As it disappeared behind the zippered flap, she noticed something at the top of the page.

*Wait…what was that first item?*

She pulled the report back out and took a closer look. It was probably a mistake; another single "open door" item logged, but this time with a keycard ID. The time stamp: 5:45 am.

*Right, which one?*

Rachel's strange double awakening on her first morning in Manhattan hadn't yet been demystified, but she knew she'd sort it out eventually. Maybe this report was a big clue. Regardless of which "5:45 am" had triggered the hotel's monitoring system, someone or something had opened and closed her suite's entry door. Is that why she awoke with a start, her heart nearly pounding out of her chest? Or was the system timestamp generated the second time when the wake up call came through?

A wave an anxiety passed thru her. She was running out of time and there was more work to do. After scrawling a brief addendum to her cryptic notes, she put the report back into the garment bag and grabbed her laptop.

Definitely in work mode now, the dining table had morphed into a classier imitation of her cubicle back at headquarters. She was what they called a "piles" person, her assigned cases neatly organized into visible stacks so that she wouldn't lose track of anything. The piles on the room's dining table were smaller, but undoubtedly more intriguing.

After establishing a VPN connection to the cloud, she entered the URL from the printout Grayson had given her at Zabars. Throughout the morning, even in the midst of her surreal adventure on the way back from the teahouse, Rachel had caught snippets of the news buzz about social media outages. Things were bad. So bad, she noticed the hotel staff manually tracking work schedules, reservations, and guest activity bookings. Despite the inconvenience, the hotel staff was adapting. They were actually talking to each other. And laughing. Could it be they were getting to know each other for the first time?

*Huh…maybe a silver lining. Whoa…*

The data readout screen display seemed to be showing that

the rogue activity had increased to triple the activity level of the day before: possibly quadruple. She'd expected it to be bad, but this was over the top. When she looked at it the day before, the rogue transmissions represented about 10% of the total. Today they represented something closer to 40%. She needed to find out what was going on in the world. She grabbed the remote and clicked on the television.

*That's strange…*

A news station was on, but it wasn't a US news station. The anchors were speaking in Arabic. Was it a clue to the mysterious identity of the overzealous housekeeping crew? If it was, it still might not mean much. There was a large contingent of Arabic speaking hotel staff, some of who could be part of the housekeeping staff. Still, she wasn't one to set aside clues based upon the benefit of the doubt. She was a digger, confirming and validating to the point of certainty. Anything still unclear meant she still had questions.

Rachel turned the station to CNN's 24 hour news cycle, knowing they'd be running regular updates, and then turned back to her work. Her ears would perk up to any relevant reports.

The hyperactive transmission activity displayed on the data readout was mesmerizing, but for some reason, she wasn't able to focus on the data. There was something about the data readout interface itself. It felt different. Along the top of the screen, a whole new set of analytical tools and utilities were now enabled. They hadn't been there the day before. And then she remembered. The group of four said she would have what she needed when she needed it.

Rachel recognized the app itself was pretty amazing. Who would develop an app like this? How was it even possible? You'd need to have a satellite view of sorts, a view that transcends and encompasses the world's global networks and satellite operations. Or you'd have to have a way of accessing every virtual security door of every social media platform in the world.

*Full circle. That's what that is.*

She gasped. *Or is it?*

Rachel wondered why she hadn't seen it before. The group of four must already have a key. Or *the* key to all doors. And the key around Mrs. Priestly's neck? It was incomplete, only partially effective. An imposter key of sorts. Priestly and her horde were determined to harness a power equal to the key held by…whom? The group of four? She reflected on her last meeting beyond the elevator. The sound of the symphony, the brilliant light, and something rising up behind Mr. Randal.

Her chair began shaking. It was her heart, pounding against the inside of her chest.

"Oh no, not this again." Images of people, places, and incidents from the past two days began converging. It wasn't complete, but the disparate parts of the larger whole, the loose ends bumping around in the back of her mind for most of the last two days, were slowly moving together into something that…made sense? Does it make sense? She wasn't sure it was the right question. Maybe the better question was "Does it shed light?"

As she studied the images forming in her mind's eye, Rachel realized that the power to see everything in virtual space, free from the limiting perspectives of proprietary network paths and secured infrastructure, was sitting right there on her laptop's screen.

It was the path to acquiring ultimate control.

Which is exactly what *Virtual Life* wants.

She pushed herself away from the table, shaking, nearly

hyperventilating with excitement and fear, emotions lifting her into a surreal awareness of a transcendent reality more powerful than anything Priestly could imagine. Or maybe Rachel wasn't giving her enough credit. Maybe Priestly knew exactly what this was about.

The CNN anchor's voice broke in. "And we have David Simpson with the latest on the social media debacle. David, what can you tell us about this morning's catastrophic termination of service in the UK?"

"Well Bob, at this moment the UK is cut off from the rest of the world. There is zero social media connectivity and, as you and I both know all too well, social media has become much more than the name implies. Global corporations, including ours, rely upon it for mission critical functions. Without access to these platforms, whole organizations, their affiliate partners, and their customers could suffer dire consequences. The amount of time and the effort required to shift to old systems or manual processes is significant. Unless a solution is implemented within the next few hours, we could see catastrophic effects on world markets, let alone significant disruption to societal norms."

Rachel felt the color drain from her face.

*Running out of…time? No. As long as they don't get the key case, we still have time.*

*Chapter Eight*

# NEW DIGS

T he clock's hands stood at 2:00 pm. Time to get moving. Rachel had 30 minutes to freshen up, arrange for a room change with Amir, and be in a cab headed to Tribeca. She felt rushed. But then, what was she thinking? Time had defied the clock since she'd arrived in Manhattan, so why try to force fit a to-do list into the space between points A and B on the face of a clock?

Rachel wasn't sure if Amir was covering the concierge podium right then. She didn't want to push her luck and make another "Concierge" call from the room phone without knowing whether Amir would pick up. And since apparently too many people knew her room number, she didn't want to leave the room vacant.

*Wait...I think I have Charles' cell number.*

Sure enough, she still had Charles' text of instructions for opening the doorman's lockbox.

"Door Services. This is Charles."

"Charles, this is Patricia Wheaton," Rachel said.

"Yes, Ms. Wheaton. How may I assist you?" Charles asked.

"Charles, would you please deliver a message to Amir?"

"Certainly. I saw him a few moments ago near the elevators. It should be no problem."

"Oh good. Please let him know that it's time. He'll know what it's about," she said.

"Yes, ma'am. Consider it done. Is there-"

"Yes...two things. First, would you please send me a text letting me know you made contact with Amir? And second, I need a cab at 2:30. If you could make sure there's one available for me, that would be great."

"Of course, Ms. Wheaton. Is there anything else?" Charles asked.

"I'm sorry. Just one more thing."

"Yes?"

"How are you?"

Charles chuckled. "I've never been better. All is well with me, Ms. Wheaton. All is well. I'll be sure to send you a text confirming contact with Amir. Have a wonderful afternoon."

"Thanks Charles...as always."

"You're very welcome."

Having Charles deliver the message would save her time fussing around the hotel looking for Amir. Gathering up her piles into neatly binder-clipped packages, she slipped them back into the compartment of her garment bag along with her laptop.

She felt a little grungy after her near-collision with the pavement, so she took a three minute shower, freshened up her hair and makeup, and put on a nice pant suit. Just as she closed the lid of her repacked suitcase, there was a knock on the door.

*Oh...I need to get the key case.*

Rachel walked out into the living area and over to the large picture window. The beautiful aubergine warp sateen drapes had been opened that morning by the housekeeping staff, but the drapery tie backs were stationary, never disturbed by the repeated opening and closing of the panels. She'd made sure of that. Grabbing hold of the left panel's tie back, she carefully removed the key case from the back of the black ornamental medallion, and slipped it into her suit pocket.

She checked her phone for the expected text. Sure enough, Charles had come through, but she wanted to be sure. Quietly tiptoeing to the door, she peeked through the peep hole and saw Amir's gentle face. He'd brought an extra large bellman cart. She swung the door open.

"Good afternoon, Amir. Please come in. I have everything ready to go."

Amir pulled the cart into the room. "I've arranged for you to stay in one of the larger suites on a higher floor. You'll be very comfortable, I guarantee. I also took the liberty of registering the room under another name," Amir said.

Rachel gathered her bags and, with Amir's help, loaded them onto the cart. "Good thinking, my friend. Good thinking. I guess I should know what it is, right? What name did you use?"

"Deborah Hancock."

Rachel dropped her carry-on, the contents of an unzipped side pocket spilling out onto the floor. She stooped down and picked up her personal items, quickly stuffing them back into the bag. Her face felt hot.

"I'm sorry, I should have talked to you first, but I had to make a quick decision. I thought it would be a good thing… a reminder of why what you're doing is so important."

"Amir, that's my mother's maiden name. Her name! Why would you do that to me?" The rush of memories flooded in. "Damn it. I wish you wouldn't have done that," she said, speaking low and controlled.

"Rachel, I'm sorry. I didn't mean to hurt you. My intention was good. We've joined forces, right? I want to save my friend Syed. And you…you want to find the people who murdered your parents."

Rachel's temper flared, but she knew he was right. The signs had been there from the beginning. This wasn't just another assignment. This was about her. It was about dealing with the past and facing whatever it was she was meant to face through the experience.

"Amir, understand me. I have to stay focused. My stomach is in knots right now. I mean, you're probably right. I know I need to deal with some things. But know this, Amir. You've crossed a line. You better not betray me. If you betray me, it won't be good."

Amir's eyes looked pained at her words. "Rachel, we're in this together. You can trust me."

"I want to, Amir. But that's easier said than done. You don't know what I've been through."

"I'm sorry." Amir finished loading the cart. "I really do understand. Remember, I loved them too." He stopped and turned to look at her. "I'll just have to prove to you that I'm trustworthy." He nodded. "Now, you must go soon. Let's head up to the new room."

Rachel huffed, managed a tiny smile and left the room. She

was agitated, the anger pushing the adrenaline into her arms and legs. "I need to do a room check."

She walked slowly, making every effort to be present to what she was doing, a technique she sometimes used to regain her composure. The en suite, the bedroom, closet, and drawers were all clear. She went back out to the living area and realized she'd forgotten something.

"Oh, dang it. I forgot the kitchen. I'm out of time. Amir, could you…?"

"Absolutely. I'll take care of it. We should go now…it's getting late."

The hallway was quiet, the elevator car empty. Amir inserted a second security card into a slot on the control panel and pressed the button for the 28th floor. The car began its ascent. Rachel wondered if they'd make it to the room. Stranger things had happened in the past two days.

The car stopped, the doors opened, and it looked like a normal hotel hallway. Amir pulled the luggage cart out and proceeded down the hall to a room situated on an outside-facing corner of the building, the spot typically reserved for larger suites. He held the door open, motioning for Rachel to step inside. The suite was more like a large apartment, the sight line from the door extending straight through to an incredible view of the city with an excellent perspective on the Empire State Building.

"Oh my gosh. This is gorgeous!"

"Yes, it's one of our luxury executive suites. It's quite a bit larger than the suite you were in, and there's added security in place that prohibits unauthorized people from gaining access to the floor. You'll be safe here."

Rachel wanted to stay, wishing her meeting with Grayson could be held in her new digs.

*It's like a beautiful hideaway in the sky.*

"I'm going to go back down to the other room and retrieve the groceries. Here's your key and your security card. I don't expect you to be here when I get back, so I'll say farewell for now," Amir said. He looked hopeful she might forgive him.

"I don't know what to say, Amir. Thank you. I'd like to take a quick look around before I go," Rachel said.

"Of course. I'll be on my way now. Have a very productive afternoon," Amir said before pulling the door halfway closed, and then stopping.

"Rachel, I'm really sorry I upset you. I hope you will forgive me," he said, searching her face for a hopeful sign.

"Amir, I need some time. I forgive you, but I need some time. Don't worry, it will be okay," Rachel said. Amir nodded, closed his eyes for a moment, and then left, closing the door behind him.

The room shone brilliantly in tasteful luxury. Always a sucker for the finer things, she felt right at home. The clock's hands were at 2:20 pm. She had five minutes to decide what to do with her precious cargo. The unpacking of her suitcases would have to wait.

*Chapter Nine*

## TO TRIBECA

The suite seemed to have no end, drawing her eye across grand spaces to cozy sitting areas peeking from behind corners, beckoning for her company. Beyond an opulent living room adjacent to a full chef's kitchen, she discovered a second bedroom and a small office. The place was bigger than most Manhattan apartments, at least the ones she could afford.

The luxury of the master bedroom overwhelmed her as she entered. Walking directly to the closet, Rachel wanted to see what sort of hotel safe it might contain. At this point she didn't have many options for securing her laptop and research materials. Inside the closet door, hidden behind several plush hotel robes, she discovered an oversized safe. It was high-end, equipped with fingerprint and retina scanning in addition to a dynamic combination that could be set to a unique code of up to 8 digits.

*This will do for now.*

Rachel grabbed the garment bag off the bellman's cart and folded it in half before setting it on the middle shelf of the safe. In her other room she'd hidden the key case "in plain sight" behind the drapery tieback medallion, but she wasn't yet familiar enough with this room to know where to hide it. She would have to either carry it with her or leave it in the safe. To hide it in the other room, she had attached the key case to a magnet and then stuck it to the back of the metal drapery medallion. The case still had the magnet attached to it, which would allow her to place it on the inside ceiling of the safe. Even if someone broke into her suite while she was gone, they might not find it. Might not.

Without enough time to thoroughly investigate the room, she wasn't comfortable taking a chance. She'd have to carry the key case on her person. Rachel grabbed her bag, pulling her weapon out to do a quick safety check and then put it back. At least she was armed if anything came up. Rachel took her jacket off and slipped the case into the interior pocket. She hung the bag across her body and put her jacket back on over it. She checked the mirror.

*Nope. Not too catawampus. Access to weapon? Check.*

The hallway was quiet. The floor seemed eerily empty and still for a low vacancy hotel. The carpet muffled the sound of her footsteps and the walls absorbed the hardly audible sound of her own breathing. An ambient light coming from no discernible source illuminated her path as she walked toward the bank of elevators. It was weird, but she wasn't afraid, although the idea of entering the elevator alone was a little off-putting. Who knew where the elevator might take her this time?

*It doesn't matter. I'm not racing down 28 flights of stairs just to get all sweaty.*

The doors opened without a sound. If she hadn't been paying attention to the lights above the doors, she wouldn't have noticed the elevator's arrival. She slid the security card Amir had given her into the slot and pushed the Main Floor button. The elevator didn't move. She tried again, but still no movement. Just as she tried a third time, the doors opened and the din of the lobby came pouring in.

*Okay. That's weird.*

Rachel exited the elevator and walked past the concierge podium, glancing over to see if Amir was working the stand. No; it was someone else. She could see Charles standing just outside the front doors, waiting beside a Lincoln Town Car. Obviously he was busy with another guest, so she waited.

"Ms. Wheaton. Good afternoon," Charles called out. He opened the passenger door and motioned for her to come over.

"I'm so sorry, I wasn't able to find a cab for you. Hopefully this will do," Charles said. He stood there, looking a little goofy, grinning a bit too wide.

"Charles, really. You're pretty funny. And very good at your job!" Rachel said. "Really, this wasn't necessary. A cab would have been just fine."

"Yes, I have no doubt you would have been fine with a cab, but I felt compelled to find a good driver; someone I know and trust," Charles said.

"Oh…I see. I hadn't really thought about it, but I understand why you did what you did. Charles. Charles Bannister. You're a good egg," Rachel said as she got into the car.

"Thank you, Ms. Wheaton. The feeling is mutual. The driver's name is Peter. He's a very good and reliable man. And he's my son." Charles shut the door and stepped back. "Have a good afternoon, Ms. Wheaton."

Rachel waved goodbye and settled back into the soft leather passenger seat. The young man looked up at her in the rearview mirror and smiled.

"Hello, Peter. My name is Patricia. It's nice to meet you."

"The pleasure is all mine, Ms. Wheaton. My father told me about you," the driver said.

"Oh really. What, pray-tell, did he say?"

"That you're smart, you have courage, and you do very important work. And that I need to make sure you get to your destination safe and sound," the driver said.

"Well, your father's a good man. And I very much like your plan."

## Chapter Ten

# NONE

*"How beautiful this dappled, soft hour of light, and yet heartbreaking. Grey at the temples, the hour of None is melancholy, a time to ponder things we thought would always be with us. The loss of our plans, our parents, our pains have eroded confidence in the ability to conquer time. . . .We crave contact with something transcendent at this time of day precisely because temporal things are dissolving into shadow."*[3]

The skies were overcast, a sticky humidity promising to do a real number on her hair. The breeze came up a few times, prompting Peter to crack his window, inviting in a gust or two of cool air. It felt good, awakening her to a stirring anticipation. She was looking forward to putting together the plan with Grayson's help. They had a lot to talk about.

"I estimate the trip at about 30 minutes. We'll take 2nd Avenue most of the way there and then cut over to Broadway at East 9th. It's the fastest route this time of day. A cab would probably get you there faster; these cabbies have their way of navigating through the congestion. I used to be a cabbie, you know. Met a lot of interesting people..." Peter said.

"Is that right? I bet you did. I've met some interesting people here too. And that's just since yesterday morning." Rachel didn't mind the chit chat. It kept her from going too far afield in her thoughts.

"Wow, that was fast. Freakishly fast! I should drive you more often! We're almost there, Ms. Wheaton. Reade is just a few blocks ahead. Incredible time. Looks like we'll pull up to the building right at 3 pm."

"Thank you, Peter. I appreciate it." The whole "time" thing was clearly beyond her, but seemed to be working in her favor.

"It's my pleasure, Ms. Wheaton. I'll be waiting outside to take you back when you're ready to return to The Kimberly."

Rachel wasn't so sure having Peter wait for her was a good idea. It could be a long planning session, and then dinner to follow. "Peter, I'd hate for you to have to wait for me. I don't know how long I'll be. How about this? I have your father's cell phone number. I can text him when I'm ready to leave. How's that?"

"As you wish, Ms. Wheaton. And thank you," Peter said.

The car pulled up in front of the building, and as it came to a stop, a sudden and unexpected wave of dread washed over her. Then, a profound grief. She looked at the streets around them and then up at the buildings.

*Where's it coming from?*

She searched the area for someone in distress, or an incident in progress, remnants of a fire...something.

"Peter, do you sense something strange...I mean, do you feel something in the air?" Rachel asked.

"I always feel it when I'm down here," Peter said, glancing up at her in the rearview mirror. He was quiet for a moment. "My dad told me that you're very perceptive. I think it might be..."

"Might be what? What is it?"

And then she saw it.

The skyline of missing towers.

"We're a few blocks from the 911 Memorial Site," Peter said.

"Oh." Something welled up inside, while something else gave way. She felt herself close up. Peter got out of the car and came around to open Rachel's door. It was as if he knew she wasn't quite herself, taking some extra time to walk with her into the lobby and then stay while they waited for Grayson to come down and meet them. Grayson stepped off the elevator less than a minute after the doorman's call to his apartment.

As soon as she saw Grayson's face, Rachel came back to herself. Smiling broadly, she made the introduction. "Mr. Raphael, this is Peter. He drove me over from the hotel. He's actually Charles' son."

"Really! Well, it's a pleasure to meet you, Peter," Grayson said, shaking Peter's hand.

"Nice to meet you too, sir. A great pleasure. I'm a huge fan of *Virtual Life*. Well, I'll be going now. Ms. Wheaton, please text my father when you're ready and I'll be here in a jiffy."

"I will, Peter. Thank you so much," Rachel said, following him outside with Grayson behind her. Peter jogged the last few feet to the car, got inside, and drove away, leaving Rachel and Grayson standing outside gazing in silence at the skyline. After a long minute, Grayson took her by the elbow, signaling it was time to go.

"I know. It's difficult the first few times you see it, but eventually you realize it's part of who we are. Come on...we've got work to do," Grayson said.

She walked quickly to get inside and escape the chill of the air. The lobby was warm with natural wood beams accented in stainless steel, creating an eclectic feel of modern homeyness. That, and the fact that it was at least 15 degrees warmer inside, was comforting. The elevator arrived within seconds of Grayson's call, and the two sped their way to the 20th floor. The doors opened to a dimly lit, yet elegant corridor.

"Wow, this place is really nice. It's so new...of course," Rachel said.

"It was built in 2012. It's a nice building...nice people. Very friendly. They're different now. I don't know why I know that. They have a unique demeanor about them. One that tells a story."

Stepping inside Grayson's apartment was like finding herself on the bright road to heaven's gate. The natural light held a commanding presence. It was no wonder: the apartment's windows spanned the entire breadth of each outside wall, stopping only at one corner where a beautiful wood pillar had been built, serving double duty as a frame for the windows and a support for a large hand-crafted table. The table had obviously been set as their working space for the afternoon. At one end was a tray set of hot tea and coffee along with a fresh fruit plate and water crackers.

"This is lovely. What a nice space to work in," Rachel said.

She was doing the best she could. She'd grieved for months after 911, obsessing over the details of the crimes leading up to the terrible acts, mourning for the victims, and battling against the temptation to become fearful, or worse yet, lose hope. Her country, the one that had been so good to her when she had had no one else, suffered a traumatic wounding that day. Ever since, it had moved further into hiding, confused and no longer sure of itself.

Rachel missed how things had been before 9/11. Even though she was placed in the foster system after her parents' murder, she had to take care of herself. It was difficult digging out of the system without any family support, but she managed with the help of employers willing to give her a chance, school administrators who saw potential, and the training and experience she received in the service. She was alone, but she'd been helped along by a cloud of witnesses cheering for her as she cleared each hurdle.

That collective optimism had eroded since 9/11. She didn't notice it at first, but now it was obvious. Trust didn't come as easily as it once did. And it wasn't just that. She felt a free-floating anger in the air. The old world, the world she'd been able to trust and rely upon for her very survival, had disappeared.

"You seem a little somber."

"Yes. 'Somber' is a good word. I'll be alright."

"It's tough to see, I know. But is there something else?" Grayson asked.

"No...no. There's nothing else. It hit me pretty hard. I still carry a tender wound about the whole thing. It changed my view of the world. I like my old world better."

"I know. Me too," Grayson said, looking pretty somber himself. "Forgive my poor manners. Please come in and sit down. I've set up-"

"Yes, I see that. It's lovely," Rachel said as she took one of the chairs at the table. "What about you? Is there something else for you? I noticed you seemed distant…kind of sad…earlier today in the meeting. Is everything alright?" Rachel asked.

Grayson's face went flush, his eyes glassy. He sat down across from her.

Rachel realized she may have overstepped. "I'm sorry, I don't mean to pry. Please. Just tell me to back off if you don't want to talk about it."

"You're not prying. There is something," Grayson whispered. He took a few breaths, unable to speak. "It's my mother. Something happened to her a few years ago, and I'm afraid she's getting worse."

"Oh my, I'm so sorry. Is she ill? How can I help?" Rachel asked.

"Oh no, it's not a health issue. I wish it were that simple." Grayson wasn't able to speak for a few moments.

"My mother lost her way. You might say that she's gone to the other side."

"What do you mean 'other side'?"

Grayson looked as if he wanted her to read his mind instead of him having to speak it out. His brow was furrowed and his jaw looked tight. Whatever he was about to say, she needed to absorb it, and for his sake, absorb it well.

"My mother's working against what you and I are working for."

Rachel instantly saw the face of Victoria Priestly, hunching like a vulture in Versace, eyeing everyone at the table as she spewed her dictates. Grayson stared at Rachel, reading her thoughts.

*That can't be right.* "Are you telling me…?"

"Yes." Grayson looked away, unable to hide his pain.

"Your mother's Victoria Priestly?" Rachel asked.

Grayson nodded.

"Bloody hell," Rachel whispered.

[3]*Praying the Hours in Ordinary Life: (Art for Faith's Sake)*
*Lauralee Farrer and Clayton J. Schmit*

## Chapter Eleven

# A GRACE GIVEN

"L et's go outside on the balcony for a second. I need some air," Grayson said.

"Yeah. Me too." Even though she hid it well, Rachel felt anxious. Why would Priestly pretend not to know Grayson? And Grayson not know her? What kind of crazy tangled web of deceit was this? She didn't understand.

Without a word, Rachel followed Grayson through the balcony doors and onto a beautiful outdoor patio furnished with a table, small fire pit, and several upholstered lounge chairs. Grayson sat down. Rachel chose the chair directly across from him. She wanted to launch an aggressive interrogation, but something held her back. Emotions were running high for both of them and her inclination toward silence in crisis compelled her to be quiet. Several minutes passed before either spoke.

"I know you have questions. I'm not very good at explaining this. It's still confusing. I understand she's extremely off-putting. My mother is a brilliant woman. It's what made her so successful before, and what makes her so dangerous now. Honestly, I can't help but wonder…"

Rachel waited. He looked unsure. Maybe he didn't want to say anything that might make it worse. "It's all right. We don't know," she said.

"That's right…we don't know…not yet."

Rachel detected a hesitance in Grayson's voice. She knew the feeling; wanting to avoid the hurt, pushing hope aside for fear of disappointment.

"I don't know what to say. Of course, I have questions. Lots of them. But I'm not sure what to do right now." She paused, gazing out across the sky to the two towers missing.

Grayson suddenly leaned forward in his chair. "How about we do what I always do?"

"What's that?"

"Throw ourselves into our work. Let's go back inside and see how far we get. I'll get the tea kettle going," Grayson said as he rose from the chair. "It's chilly out here!"

"I'll be there in a minute," Rachel said. She couldn't take her eyes off the skyline. For the first time since she'd arrived, she felt afraid. She didn't know why she felt afraid, exactly. Maybe it was the chilling audacity of *Virtual Life* to presume a place of dominance over the world's main method of communication. Yeah…that was probably it. What else could it be?

The temperature was dropping, the shadows lengthening as they always did around that time in the afternoon. The 3 o'clock hour beckoned her to ponder things she'd once thought would be with her forever. Melancholy had started moving in.

*No no no…no time for that. There's too much to do right now.*

Rachel opened the door and stuck her head in. "May I come in now?"

Grayson looked up, the familiar twinkle in his eye. He understood her attempt at levity. "Of course, come right in Ms. Vaughn. Please join me at the table."

"Thank you, kind sir." Rachel cleared her throat. "Grayson, there were some interesting developments today. May I do a quick brain dump with you first, just to get us both up to speed?"

"Absolutely, let's do it. Here you go…I selected a tea for you. I hope you like Ginger Peach," Grayson said, setting the steaming cup down in front of her.

"That's my favorite, thank you. Okay, first, after you dropped me off, I had tea with Amir at a little place a few blocks from the hotel."

Rachel began relaying the conversation to Grayson. He listened closely, but he didn't seem surprised that Amir and Syed were friends. He also didn't react to the news that Amir and Syed had worked with her parents.

"Grayson, why do I get the feeling you already knew all this before I told you?" Rachel asked.

Grayson smiled and let out a nervous chuckle. "Okay, you got me. I knew a little bit, but not everything. Let me put it this way. It's like I've known what you data geeks call the 'meta' data, but not the actual data itself. A lot of what you're telling me is news, but none of it is a surprise. For example, I knew Mr. Randal had made contact with Amir, but I didn't know why."

"I see." Rachel paused, her mind firing off several more questions before settling on one.

"Are you okay?" Grayson asked.

71

"Processing. Please wait."

Grayson snorted, her retort obviously tickling his funny bone and triggering a cathartic belly laugh. She couldn't help laughing herself.

"Okay...okay...sorry. I didn't mean that to be funny."

"It's cute! Don't apologize," Grayson said. "Go ahead, ask away."

Rachel took a deep breath. "Okay, Grayson. Who am I to you?"

Grayson was taken aback by her question, but didn't seem completely unprepared for it.

"Wow, what a question. From what I can tell, I think that... uh, let's see. How do I say this?" He paused, looking up at a corner of the room. "I think...that you're my given grace."

His response nearly took her breath away.

"What exactly do you mean by that?" Rachel asked. She studied him, wanting to know if he was feeding her a line or not. She'd fallen for smart and attractive men before, but all her relationships had either abruptly ended in heartbreak or died from her intellectual boredom.

"Mr. Randal and the people with him...I know this is obvious. They're more than what they appear to be. I'm not saying I know exactly who they are, but when it comes to me, they have always provided what I need when I need it. I've never had to ask. And it's not just in terms of getting the job done. It's also what *I* need. What I need emotionally and spiritually. It's like they're looking out for my soul. Before I received this assignment, I thought that part of my life was over; my mother was gone. We had been close..."

Grayson's voice trailed off. Rachel felt it; a slightly familiar strain of pain.

"As the assignment went on and she began harassing me, I started to struggle. I never said anything about it, but then you showed up. The timing couldn't have been more perfect."

"Grayson, I think I understand." Rachel thought about it before continuing. "Maybe we're kindred spirits. Maybe it's one of the reasons we've been brought together. I feel like you're a grace given for me too; a comforter…a source of strength and courage."

Grayson sat back, his face glowing as the words washed over him.

"I don't understand much, but I think I see a little bit of what's going on here," Rachel said, wagging two fingers back and forth between them.

Grayson got a mischievous look on his face. "Would you like to dance?"

"What? It's 3:30 in the afternoon! Don't you think we ought to get to work?"

It was too late. Grayson had already turned on the music, and *Junior Walker and The All-Stars* had taken center stage. She'd always wanted to do some old-school dance moves to *Shotgun*.

"All right. One dance. But that's it!"

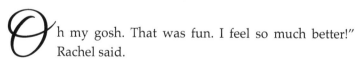

*O*h my gosh. That was fun. I feel so much better!" Rachel said.

"Girl, you can move! You're great. Let's have another," Grayson said between gasps for air.

Rachel took her jacket off, careful to check that the key case was safe and sound in the interior pocket. She was anxious to finish the brain dumping process.

"I'd love to, but not now. There's more I need to tell you."

Grayson nodded and motioned her to the table, unable to speak while he caught his breath.

"Dang, Grayson. That was nothing! You need to get into shape," Rachel said, teasing him a little.

"Yeah. Okay, Frannie Fitness." Grayson said.

"Ha ha, very funny. All right, we need to focus. I need to tell you more about today."

"Okay, shoot."

"Something happened as I was leaving the tea house today. When I stepped out onto the sidewalk, I was shoved. Hard. I started falling face first into the concrete but managed to break my fall. Then someone pulled me up. When I turned around there was no-one there. I swear I felt it...a hand around my upper arm, pulling me up as if I were as light as a feather."

Grayson poured his hot tea into a glass of ice cubes. "Do you want yours iced?"

"Did you hear what I said?" Rachel asked, wondering why Grayson looked so nonchalant.

"Yes, of course. I listen to every word you say." Grayson said. "That's a little weird, I'll give you that."

"Is this just standard fare in your world? Invisible hands helping you out of a bad spot?"

"Uh...yeh."

Rachel scowled. Grayson was a little too coy with whatever information he had. But that was fine. She'd play along.

"Okay, then how about this? Whoever bumped into me apologized, but I didn't see who it was. The foot traffic was too heavy to pick him out of the crowd. So I waited, thinking there was a good chance he would turn around and look."

"Good strategy. Impressive."

"Stop. I'm serious. This is a serious incident. Anyway, all of a sudden it was like someone had pressed a button. The people walking went into slow-motion, and the lights went dim. It got pretty dark. The only source of light was from an area about 50 yards away in the direction of whoever shoved me."

"Okay, now I'm intrigued," Grayson said.

"That's not all. Then the crowd parted, and a path opened up down the middle of the sidewalk. A man standing at the end of the path turned around and looked at me. As soon as he did, I couldn't see anything. I'd gone blind."

Grayson shed his nonchalant demeanor and seemed to be paying closer attention to her story, his piercing eyes squinting as if his thoughts could only race while she spoke.

"Then, a second later, my sight came back. He was still standing there looking at me." Rachel felt her chest get tight. She started breathing faster. "Sorry…this is weird." She took in a deep breath and continued. "His face had a soft glow to it. I felt like we were alone, just him and me. I didn't know what to make of it. He looked familiar."

"You've seen him before? Recently?"

"Yeah…very recently. I keep wanting to place him in the conference room at *Virtual Life*, but not at the table. Really, I've been wracking my brain trying to remember. You were there. Do you have any idea who he might be?"

Grayson sat still: no blinks, no body movement. Just a blank stare. *Is he even breathing?*

"Are you okay?"

He abruptly leaned forward. "What else?" Grayson asked, his voice carrying an intensity she hadn't heard before.

"What do you mean, what else?"

"What else happened?"

"I yelled out to him, but as soon as I did, everything went back to normal time. And the lights went back on. I lost him in the crowd. I tried to find him again, but he was gone. Next thing I knew, Charles is there with my coat. We walked back to the hotel together."

"Where was Amir all this time?"

"He was still in the teahouse buying tea to bring home."

Grayson stared at Rachel. She wasn't sure what he was thinking, but it definitely wasn't anything romantic or playful. He looked calm, yet sober; very sober. The apartment went quiet as if someone had turned off the sounds of the city below. And as the two of them waited, a full silence blanketed the room.

*Chapter Twelve*

# THE PITCH

G rayson went into the den to get his portfolio containing the staff roster and candidate resumes. Rachel took the last sip of tea while thinking through different strategies for pitching their proposal to the execs the next morning. It was getting late and even though they'd already covered a lot of ground, the mountain of work in front of them felt daunting. They only needed one simple and elegant solution, one that nobody in their right mind would object to. Those kinds of solutions were the hardest to define; she often found that people make things more complicated than they need to be.

"Earth to Rachel. Where are you?" Grayson said as he walked back into the living area.

"Oh. Sorry. I was thinking about how we're going to pitch this. We don't want to leave any room for an objection on Priestly's... Sorry. Mrs. Priestly's part. It's paramount that we get beyond the job offer and start establishing the team; a team that includes Syed Haddad. I suspect he's our key to learning how *Virtual Life* has been causing all these disruptions to service. No pun intended."

Grayson looked preoccupied. "It's all right. You can call her Priestly. That's what I call her. Anyway, to me, she's not the same person. And yes, I agree with you about Syed Haddad."

Rachel was reminded of Grayson's vulnerability. He sat down and placed the staff roster on the table in front of her alongside a pile of resumes. "Syed's is the first resume on the stack," Grayson said.

They worked through the roster, selecting six possible candidates for what she thought would be a three or four person team. Two were from Calista Lawrence's division, including Syed Haddad, and the other four were from George Kendall's organization. It was a relief to finish the tedious part of the afternoon's work.

"Great. That's done. Remember, Trader made a commitment to make Syed available for an interview, so this shouldn't be a problem. But we need to make sure they only have one option when we select him. Approve."

"I like it. But I'm also getting hungry. What time do you want to break for dinner? We can talk strategy over a fine piece of halibut. And maybe a glass of wine…and a little dessert," Grayson said, nudging her elbow a little as he spoke.

"Dinner sounds fabulous. How about 5? That gives us almost an hour to finish comparing notes."

"Party pooper."

"Hey! We've got work to do-" Rachel suddenly remembered she hadn't told Grayson about Calista Lawrence's unannounced visit. "Good grief, how could I forget? I had an unexpected visitor today…Calista Lawrence. She came pounding on my hotel room door."

"Pounding?"

"Yeah…pounding and then that fast incessant knocking that makes you nervous."

"Really." Grayson narrowed his eyes and smirked as if running a stream of possible theories through his mind. "That's very interesting. What'd she want?" he asked.

"I don't know. I didn't answer the door. I wasn't about to let her in without knowing why she was there or how she knew my room number. She was obviously upset about something. Inviting her in would have been too risky, not to mention bad form for a pro like me. Anyway, I managed to sneak a phone call to Amir. Charles came up to the floor to find out what was going on and when he got there, I heard her try to finagle her way inside by claiming to be my mother. Charles was having none of her nonsense. He escorted her out. For all I know, he eighty-sixed her from the joint."

"You know, as refined and educated as you are, sometimes I feel like I'm talking to some tough street-wise chick," Grayson said.

"Yeah, well sometimes it comes out. I've had some colorful seasons in my life."

Grayson nodded in an understanding way. "It's kind of cool."

"Stay focused…please," Rachel said.

Grayson sat up straight. "So, Calista showed up. Interesting development. I'm not sure about her. She acts like she's 'all in' on whatever game *Virtual Life* is playing in the market. But once in a while the sparks really fly between her and my mother…er, Priestly. Did you notice that in the meeting today?"

Rachel laughed. "How could I not? I've been thinking a lot about it. Calista is Syed's direct boss. Today she said he's being considered for a transfer, and then Priestly interrupted her to say Syed could be made available. Calista didn't look very happy. Kind of ticked off. There's definitely something going on there."

"Yeah, you got me on that one. I rarely understand what's going on between women."

Rachel laughed. "You're a man! How could you?"

"Get to work, Ms. Vaughn."

Grayson picked up and began studying Syed's resume again when he suddenly slapped his hand down on the table. "I think I know who the man on the street might be."

Nonplussed, Rachel gasped. "You do? Who?"

"You said he looked familiar, right? Do you remember when Syed was escorted out of the room?" Rachel nodded. "A staff person was standing next to the exit door. He was wearing a uniform. Like a maintenance uniform. I noticed him because he looked out of place."

Grayson's wheels were turning, but Rachel wasn't sure he was on the right track. "I don't get it. What's the connection?" Rachel asked.

"What was the man on the street wearing?"

Rachel could hardly remember what Amir wore at the tea house, let alone the attire of a glowing-face man standing in the dark 50 yards away.

"Give me a minute. I need to switch gears," she said.

Rachel closed her eyes and began practicing a refocusing

technique she'd learned while serving in the Middle East. She breathed deeply, paying attention to different parts of her body, relaxing her muscles as she worked one by one from the bottom of her feet to the top of her head. It helped her relax enough to concentrate and allow insights and images to emerge from her subconscious.

"His attire wasn't anything unusual. There were lots of business people in the crowd...a whole bunch of suits. I don't think he was wearing a suit. At least not a nice one. It wasn't black. I remember it as dowdy, but nothing more specific. He was dressed like someone I might easily overlook," Rachel said.

"Exactly."

"Grayson, you've got something swirling. I can tell. Come on. What are you thinking?"

"I'm not sure. It's just a hunch, but I suspect the man is somehow connected with the group of four. That's it. I know this doesn't make any sense, but they're always referring to others. Not by name, but by position. Here...here's an example. Remember when you asked Mr. Randal if he was in charge and his response was that he's not 'the highest'?"

"Yes, I absolutely do. It was an interesting way of putting it."

"That's what I mean, Mr. Randal's and Ms. Florentine's ways are different; a little obscure. They speak in word pictures and use analogies that I don't always understand. It's like that phrase I heard somewhere...looking through a glass darkly where you can see something, but it's not yet clear enough to make out the details."

"Yeah, like now."

Grayson chuckled. "I know. I'm being really vague right now. I just have a hunch there's a connection, but I don't know what it is exactly. Sometimes the understanding comes to me later, usually when I'm not thinking about it."

Rachel was about to say something when Grayson interrupted. He leaned across the table and whispered.

"But I will tell you this. As I listened to you describe what happened today, I had a strong sense that we were not alone."

## Chapter Thirteen

# AN UNEXPECTED VISITOR

K *nock knock knock*

Startled, they both turned to look at the door. "Who could that be?" Rachel whispered.

"I'm not sure."

"Does anyone else know this is your apartment?"

"It's a corporate lease. A *Virtual Life* lease. I just moved in a week ago."

Rachel thought that was actually a good thing. Given they'd discussed their plans to prepare a list of candidates, it wouldn't be considered out of the ordinary for her to be there. Still, she felt the need to be cautious. Rachel gave Grayson the quiet sign and got up to get her bag from the chair. She pulled her weapon and then found a good spot just inside the entry to the den and out of sight. She quickly double-checked that the key case was still secure in her jacket pocket.

As Rachel took position, Grayson looked through the apartment door's peep hole. He turned to Rachel with eyes wide and mouthed, "It's Calista Lawrence."

She motioned him to come over. He yelled, "Just a minute!" as he walked to where Rachel was hiding.

"How do you want to play this?" Rachel asked.

"Let's see what she wants. You stay here and I'll see what's going on. I trust your judgment, so move when you think you need to."

Rachel nodded. Grayson walked back over to the door. "Coming!" He put on his best easy going Michael Raphael persona and opened the door.

"Calista! To what do I owe the pleasure of a visit from you?" Grayson asked. "Please come in."

"Thank you, Michael. Ahh…I always loved this apartment. I stayed here when I first started with *Virtual Life*. If these walls could talk…Oh, am I interrupting anything?" Calista had noticed the two cups of tea on the table.

"Well, actually, Ms. Wheaton and I are in the throes of preparing a candidate list for her team. Is there something you need?"

"And she is…?" Calista began to ask.

"She's freshening up. What can I do for you, Calista?" Grayson's voice had definitely shifted into professional Michael mode. Very commanding.

"Well, uh…gee, I'm sorry to barge in on you. I was hoping to speak with you about Syed Haddad. Confidentially of course." Calista's voice changed ever so slightly. She looked tense.

"Okay. I'm listening," Grayson said.

"May I sit down? It won't take long. I'm feeling a little woozy...probably the altitude."

"Certainly, by all means," Grayson said. Rachel slipped her weapon in her back waist band and emerged from the den.

"Oh, hello Ms. Lawrence. I wasn't expecting you to be here today," Rachel said. She gave her a half smile, not wanting Calista to think it was acceptable to interrupt their meeting. She had a reputation to build.

"Hello, Ms. Wheaton. I wasn't expecting to be here either, but my earlier efforts to contact you didn't work out," Calista said. She tried to hide her irritation, but Rachel saw through Calista's facade.

"So, Calista, Ms. Wheaton and I have a great deal of work to do. Forgive me for being direct, but why are you here?"

"Of course. I'm probably making a huge mistake, but I felt compelled to find you. After watching Ms. Wheaton's performance in the meeting today, I felt there might be some hope."

"Hope? Hope for what?" Grayson asked. Rachel wasn't buying it. She saw how crafty she'd been with Charles earlier. She figured Calista was there to pursue an alliance against Priestly.

"I can't believe I'm saying this. I'm as ambitious as the next person, but things have gotten out of hand." Calista stopped, seemingly hesitant to speak. "Veronica is leading us down a dangerous path. I wouldn't normally break protocol, but I and the rest of the executive team have become very uncomfortable. We've lost our voices, which means we've lost our power to effect a change in course."

Rachel knew it was best to let Grayson take the lead. For all Calista knew, Grayson was Michael Raphael, one of the other executives. Without missing a beat, Grayson said, "Yes,

I've noticed that too, but I decided to become better acclimated to the corporate culture before asking any questions."

"You played it well, Michael. It's a tough environment. Trader and Priestly paint an impressive picture, but their management style…well, let's just say it leaves a lot to be desired. There's very little openness; people are afraid to be candid. And for good reason."

"Really. I haven't felt that myself, but I see what you're saying. There's certainly a tension in the room. Have there been repercussions?"

"You saw what happened with Mr. Haddad," Calista said.

Grayson glanced at Rachel. She wasn't buying it, giving him a nearly imperceptible shake of the head.

Calista continued. "I'm sorry. I came here because I thought you might better prepare for tomorrow if you know what's going on. Things are heating up. My access to Mr. Haddad has been cut off and after yesterday's incident, I'm a little worried about him."

Rachel saw her opportunity. "Ms. Lawrence, is there a reason you should be worried about Mr. Haddad? Has he done something wrong?"

Calista looked at Grayson. "Michael, I'm dancing on some boundaries here. I'm not sure what I should disclose."

"Calista, the only way I'm going to consider helping you is if you tell us what you know. And then we'll forget that this meeting ever happened," Grayson said. "You need to answer Ms. Wheaton's question."

Calista looked nervous, as if she'd been caught unprepared. Rachel sensed that Calista had come to the 20th floor without a plan: a bush league mistake.

Calista cleared her throat. "Okay. I'll tell you what I know.

Mr. Haddad, like many of the other former CEOs, was pressured by *Virtual Life* to sell. Most of the others eventually acquiesced to *Virtual Life's* lead because of the money. But Mr. Haddad hasn't been as easy to manipulate. On the contrary, he's become increasingly resistant to working with my engineering group."

"I'm sorry, Ms. Lawrence. Would you remind me which organization you manage?" Rachel asked.

"My organization is responsible for developing new technologies that improve *Virtual Life's* competitive advantage," Calista said, her voice fading as she spoke.

"I see. And does your organization have anything to do with the recent catastrophic increases in social media service outages...like the one impacting the UK at this very moment?" Rachel asked.

"It's possible our work has something to do with that."

"Ms. Lawrence, don't be coy. Are you running a project that aims to disrupt the global social media space?" Rachel asked. Calista wouldn't be going anywhere until she spilled what she knew.

"We're working on projects that lead us to have greater competitive advantage," Calista said.

"So basically 'yes'," Grayson said.

Calista didn't respond.

"So, what does Mr. Haddad have to do with this project?" Grayson asked.

"Priestly placed him on our team as the senior engineer. We haven't yet been able to produce the results Priestly is demanding. Until *Virtual Life* implements a fully operational solution, the other companies can still recover and quickly restore service. Even now, the average recovery time of our competitors is shortening incrementally with each outage. Eventually, their recovery algorithms will restore service with no perceptible interruption to the customer unless we can permanently terminate their capacity for service delivery. Priestly thinks that Haddad can get us there."

"And you support this?" Rachel asked.

"Uh...no. Of course not. I mean...I didn't know. No one knew...at first. My team was asked to investigate the code embedded in a key provided to our team. We all thought it was a little strange, but we discovered that the key contained an internal storage drive, and the drive contained several encrypted files. We began working on the decryption process and managed, without Mr. Haddad's assistance, to operationalize some of the key's functionality. When we reported our findings to Trader and Priestly, they insisted we test it in a live environment."

"What do you mean, 'without Mr. Haddad's assistance?'" Rachel asked.

"Like I told you. He's resistant, so Priestly has ordered heavy hands on him. I suspect he knows more about this technology than what I was told."

"So, you're saying you've been in the dark about this?" Grayson asked.

"Like I said, only at first. It didn't take long to see the implications. And based upon Priestly's insistence on Mr. Haddad's cooperation, I think she knew all along that he's essential to us making any real progress. And he wants out."

Grayson stood up and put his hands together as if readying himself to make a speech. "Calista, you were there today when Trader made the commitment to make Mr. Haddad available. We're going to take him at his word."

Calista stopped short of rolling her eyes. "Yes, I understand."

Grayson paused, giving Calista a stern once-over.

"Uh huh." Grayson appeared to be in no rush to reassure her. "You may be telling us the truth, and then again, you may not. I've noticed some pretty regular sparks flying between you and Priestly. You can be sure that Ms. Wheaton and I will be checking out your story. If it checks out, I'll be in contact."

Calista looked down for a moment as if to consider whether she should say anything more. She cleared her throat. Looking up at Grayson, she said, "Let me offer a good faith gesture with some information. First, there is no such thing as 'private' in the *Virtual Life* building. And second, I have a question. Have you wondered why *Virtual Life* is making such an aggressive play for Ms. Wheaton?"

Grayson seemed to recognize Calista was trying to pull him in. "I think that's probably enough for tonight. Ms. Wheaton and I still have a lot of work to do. I'll show you out," Grayson said.

"Yes, I suppose it is. Ms. Wheaton? Mr. Raphael? Good evening."

Calista left. Grayson and Rachel stood quiet as the door clicked closed behind her.

*Chapter Fourteen*

# DINNER AND DATA

The table had been cleared of working materials and re-set with dinnerware. Rachel chopped vegetables for roasting while Grayson worked on a fifteen minute marinade for the halibut.

"So you don't believe her?" Grayson asked.

"It's not that I don't believe her. It's that I think she's up to something. I don't trust her. What she told us may be true, but I'm not so sure why she told us. We need to think carefully about aligning with her. Especially given that little shot at the end where she tried to rattle me with the question about why *Virtual Life* is making such a strong play for me."

"I agree. A wise woman you are," Grayson said, taking a bow in her direction.

"Thank you. Thank you very much," Rachel said in her best Elvis Presley voice.

"She did give us some good information, especially about the lack of privacy in the *Virtual Life* building. We need to request an off-site with Mr. Haddad," Grayson said.

Rachel's wheels began turning. If they succeeded in arranging an off-site, Syed could be sequestered in a secret place. If Calista's story were true, it wouldn't be improbable for him to attempt an escape. If he's really being held against his will, he might cooperate. Even Amir could help, securing a place for Syed to hide out.

"Grayson, how difficult do you think it'll be to arrange for an off-site?"

"It shouldn't be too difficult. After all, you're in the power position right now. For whatever reason, as Calista alluded, they're putting the major moves on you. I'll be surprised if they don't agree. But the meeting place has to be kept secret, and with these guys it means turning off all social media accounts, location services, etc. Anything that might allow them to trace our movements."

"Good thinking. I don't have a personal cell, but you never know."

"I don't either, but interestingly enough, today of all days the company issued a corporate cell to me. Fortunately so far I haven't been anywhere Michael Raphael ought not be. I'll need to remember to turn everything off…or better yet, just leave the phone here."

Rachel thought about running her idea by Grayson, but decided to wait to see how things unfolded with Syed. Everything would have to be just right to pull something like that off. After all, it could be painted as a kidnapping.

"How are you doing with that marinade? Do I have time to bring you up to date on one other thing?" Rachel asked.

"Of course, go ahead. We've got time. I can serve dinner whenever you're ready to eat."

"I had another interesting epiphany today," Rachel said.

"Do tell."

"I took a look at the data readout screen before I left the hotel." She waited for a reaction. He looked puzzled, but waited for her to continue. She liked that about him; he was an excellent listener.

"I had a 'duh' moment."

"For some reason you don't strike me as a 'duh' moment kind of person," Grayson said, flashing a twinkling-eye smile.

"Believe me, I've had my share. I just hide it well." She looked away, feeling a little embarrassed by her flirtatious tone. "But that's neither here nor there. The first day I was here, the day I met you, I did some analysis of the data readouts you gave me. I detected a low level of transient anomalies across the various networks; anomalies causing a number of aborted transmissions. After watching it for a while, I noticed the anomalies started as a legitimate transmission but then morphed. They went 'rogue' for lack of a better term, and became hostile, causing a small percentage of the other transmissions to abruptly terminate mid-transaction. I think this is what's causing all the outages."

"You always make things seem reasonable even though a lot of the technical stuff sounds like a lot of gobbledygook to me. And I'm not seeing the 'duh' moment." Grayson said.

"The 'duh' moment happened today. I took another look at the data readouts to see if there'd been any change. Sure enough, the rogue transmissions had increased. But here's the thing. The data readout system itself..." Rachel found herself at a loss for words.

"What? Tell me." Grayson asked.

Rachel took a deep breath. "I hate to be wrong. It's a thing with me. But as I watched the screen, I realized that what I was seeing…can't be seen." Grayson looked quizzical. "As far as I know, the scope of data displayed on the screen can't be captured and aggregated like that, not even with satellites. The technology doesn't exist. It means that whoever created the data readout system is…" She stopped.

"What? Don't leave me wondering. What do you think it means?"

"Okay. It's possible I'm behind on the latest tech breakthroughs, so I'm not absolutely sure. But to build a system like that, you'd have to be all-seeing…somehow transcendent." Rachel wondered if Grayson was following her. "Grayson, you're the one who provided the URL of the data readout system. Who gave it to you?"

"Rachel, I'm sorry, but I'm not sure I'm tracking with you. Are you talking about the recipe I printed out when we were at Zabars?" Grayson asked.

"Yes. Who gave that to you?"

"Uh…Google?"

"You didn't know what that was? That URL took me to a data readout display exactly like the displays in the room where we met with the group of four. I thought you knew that." Rachel had assumed too much. "You knew about the algorithm…the Vaughn Algorithm, so I assumed you knew about the data readouts."

"No. No, I didn't. I mean, I noticed the row of display panels in the meeting, of course, but to my eyes they showed just a bunch of pretty screen savers. I probably didn't need to see the data. You're the data geek on this team, not me. That's how things seem to work. I get what I need when I need it."

"So you're telling me that noone gave it to you. You just

randomly did a search for a recipe and that's what came up on a screen?" Rachel asked.

"Yep. You remember. I read the list of ingredients to you."

"I do remember, but at that point I wasn't sure who you were or what was going on, so I didn't ask you about the disconnect."

"Wow. A big disconnect," Grayson said.

"Yeah. It seems that way. But maybe not. You said it yourself that we only get the information we need when we need it. I needed it and, obviously, you didn't. But now we both do."

How could Grayson not have seen the readouts? Were they for her eyes only? And why her?

"I can't believe what I'm about to say. Grayson, listen to me. I saw the totality of real-time transmissions across the world's social media infrastructures all in one view. This means that the group of four already has the key. Or something like it. Better yet, the real key. And that the one Priestly wears around her neck is like a 'knock-off.' It makes sense. Think about it. When you walk into the *Virtual Life* building, all the natural light has been cut off and replaced with those super expensive lighting systems. The lighting systems themselves are beautiful to look at, but they cast harsh and unflattering shadows, unlike the beauty revealed by natural light. Just like their version of the key. They're trying to achieve the same kind of all knowing transcendence through their one-off version of the 'real' key."

Rachel put her head down on the table, her face cradled in her hands.

Grayson cleared his throat. "You know Priestly is the master mind behind this, right?"

Rachel sat up and stroked the side of her face, her mind's eye watching the pieces converge into a clearer picture. "Yes, you're right. And I think I've got our pitch for tomorrow."

"What are you thinking?" Grayson asked.

"What's the last thing Priestly would want to do right now?"

## Chapter Fifteen

# ALL AT ONCE

"**D**elicious meal, kind sir," Rachel said, smiling across the table at Grayson, who was sporting a speck of halibut near the corner of his mouth. She made the polite motion for him to wipe his face. He didn't get it. She did it again. He still didn't get it.

"Is your chin itchy?" Grayson asked.

"No. I'm trying to be polite. You have a piece of fish on your chin," Rachel said, chuckling at his momentary obtuseness.

Grayson wiped his mouth. "Did I get it?"

Rachel nodded, smiling as she chewed.

"Thanks. I did that on purpose. I didn't want you to think I was perfect."

"Uh huh. Clever guy, you are."

"Oh my gosh, it's nearly 9:30. We should probably start wrapping things up. I want to be fresh for tomorrow, don't you?" Grayson asked.

"Absolutely. I'll text Charles. He can send Peter to pick me up."

After she sent the message, Rachel cleared the plates from the table and began loading the dishwasher. Grayson did a little jog across the room and turned the sound system on. Next thing Rachel knew, *Super Freak* by *Rick James* filled the apartment.

"You've got be kidding me. *Rick James*? Good grief. All right. I'm in," Rachel said. She took off her shoes and skipped into the open area of the living room floor. Grayson jumped over an ottoman, joining her without missing a beat.

"See, isn't this great? We're working off the dessert! No guilt tomorrow morning," Grayson shouted over the music.

*Thump thump thump*

He ran to turn the volume down. "Oops...I guess it's late. Sorry, it's my neighbor upstairs. We'll have to do this another time."

"That's all right...it was one of the best 20 second dances I've ever had," Rachel said.

The apartment landline rang. "Michael Raphael. Yes, thank you. She'll be down in a few minutes."

"Is Peter here?" Rachel asked.

"Not quite yet. He called ahead to tell the doorman he's about ten minutes away. Let me make a copy of the list. You might want to study it later tonight, or whatever you do that makes you so smart." Grayson grabbed the working papers and went into the den.

Rachel considered the data readout view as impossibly transcendent, a phenomenon beyond her capacity to understand. But she also knew she needed to try with her whole heart to press into the mystery, as frightening and painful as it might be for her, and possibly for Grayson. Rachel felt a stirring within, calling her to lean into a present and profound calm. She knew something was coming her way.

Grayson came out of the den, copies in hand. "Here you go. Are you ready? I can go down with you."

"Yep, I'm ready. Thank you so much for the lovely dinner and conversation," Rachel said.

"And...?"

"And...work?" Rachel asked.

"And...?"

She wasn't tracking. Grayson smirked in exasperation.

"Oh! The dance! Thank you for the dance!"

"You're very welcome. Do you want a scarf for the ride home? It's pretty cold out there."

"Sure, that would be nice." Grayson went to the bedroom. Rachel quickly checked her purse for her weapon, and her jacket pocket for the key case. Both were in place.

"Here you go, Ms. Rachel. Ready?"

She nodded. The cooler temperature of the dimly lit hallway prompted her to put on Grayson's scarf and button her jacket. The cashmere felt soft against her neck, reminding her that she'd be spending the night in her new hotel digs. Something else to look forward to.

They proceeded down the quiet hallway, turned a corner, and entered the elevator alcove where one open car was waiting. She stepped inside with Grayson close behind, turned to face forward, and felt the interior begin its transformation as the doors closed. The smell of roses and rich mahogany filled the small space, the gold hand-railings sparkling with familiarity. She looked at Grayson, who shrugged in response to her questioning brow. The elevator car hadn't moved, yet she heard a rising and beautiful sound of music. Violins, cellos, a soft and emotional flute. The music grew louder, and then a voice. Singing. Operatic. An aria. Her thoughts went back to so many missions, strapped into her seat, waiting for take off. She'd put her headphones on and listen to *Kiri Te Kanawa* singing *Puccini*, her beautiful voice calming Rachel as she prayed through the takeoff.

"Agent Blaine, please proceed with the security protocol," said some ethereal voice. The interior went awash with light, enabling Rachel to better see Grayson move through the mesmerizing protocols he'd carried out that first time. After he finished, they waited for what felt like several minutes.

"Did you do it right?" she whispered.

Grayson put his finger up to his mouth, giving her the quiet sign. And then raised one brow, obviously exasperated that she would think to question him.

The doors opened, revealing the group of four standing just outside the elevator doors waiting for them.

"Good evening, Rachel," Ms. Florentine said. "It is always very good to see you. Please...come forward."

Ms. Florentine's eyes were magnificent, almost otherworldly. Rachel had never seen eyes so clear. *Kiri's* voice rose and dipped in smooth waves, the air pungent with a melancholy joy. She breathed in the scent of the aria emerging from her memories as it enveloped her in a warm assurance that beckoned her to move forward, Ms. Florentine all the while motioning for her and Grayson to enter their space.

They seemed different, now embodying a serenity that Rachel hadn't noticed before. Each took their place at the table, choosing seats closer to her and Grayson than during their previous two visits. The data readout displays were still on the wall, but there were more of them. Many more.

Beyond the opposite end of the long table, beautiful fabrics had been pulled back to reveal a "viewing." "Viewing" was the only word she could think of for what was before her. It wasn't a screen or a display panel. She didn't know what it was, but she couldn't stop looking at it. Someone touched her hand and she turned to see it was Grayson.

"We should probably pay attention now, don't you think?" he whispered. His attempt at humor seemed ill-timed to her, but she smiled and sat up straight.

It was quiet. Ms. Florentine, Ms. Gold, and Mr. Glass appeared to be waiting for Mr. Randal to speak. Mr. Randal stared ahead, blinking every few seconds, cocking his head one way and then the next, and pursing his lips together in concentration. Rachel watched, imagining with fascination what might be going on in Mr. Randal's consciousness. He seemed to be listening again. And then he turned to her and spoke.

"Rachel, you are here to observe," said Mr. Randal.

"Sir?" Rachel was confused.

"Observe, my dear. Pay attention," Mr. Randal said as he swept his arms up and apart as if to direct her focus toward everything at once.

She wanted to look at the "view" first, but forced herself to look around from the back of the room to the front and then down the other side, taking in all she could while remembering not to try too hard. Extraordinary effort would ruin it; she knew that. She needed to surrender to seeing what called out to her. This wasn't the moment to overanalyze and muffle the voice of insight.

As she gazed across the data readout panels, she realized that the further she looked down the wall to her left, the sharper the image, each subsequent display delivering crystal clear visuals of what appeared to be real-time transmissions. At one point she recognized a pattern she'd discovered while working as a data forensics tech a decade before. They didn't have near this quality of definition back then. It was unique and momentary, never to be repeated. Could it be video? Impossible. How could she be seeing it now as a real-time transmission? She skipped a dozen or so panels to the two displays located directly to her right.

"Oh..." Rachel gasped, took a breath, and exhaled with a slight tremble. She could feel Grayson's eyes searching her face for answers. Bizarrely, Mr. Randal began humming the melody of the aria. Rachel didn't understand what she was seeing. She wasn't afraid. It was something else.

"You're doing fine, my dear," said Ms. Florentine.

Rachel saw an aggressive array of predatory disrupters thwarting the successful completion of data transmissions. Just like what she'd seen earlier today. No. Exactly what she had seen earlier today. The same exact transmission patterns. Impossible.

Was she seeing real time transmissions that occurred today, and others occurring one moment over ten years ago...all at once?

Rachel scrutinized the data read outs, working her way down the row analyzing one display and then the next, each subsequent readout more fuzzy than the previous. She continued down the line, finding no last panel to mark the end. They continued, endless into a limitless...something. Were these future moments? Or were these predictive patterns extrapolated from historical data? That couldn't be right. It didn't explain their apparent infinitude. She stretched the capacity of her sight to the last panel that was still somewhat discernible. Big movements, shadows, and a lesser sense of furious activity. It "felt" balanced; beautiful and ordered. It was as Grayson had said: like seeing through a glass darkly.

Sitting back in her chair, she noticed Mr. Randal held an anticipatory posture, as if expecting her to continue.

"What is the meaning of this?" she asked.

Mr. Randal hummed. Ms. Florentine gestured toward the "view."

The view had an odd movement about it. Images faded in and out, all conveying intimately familiar thoughts and memories. An elderly woman, covering an infant with a beautiful handmade quilt. A young father sitting near a window, staring off across a city with a faraway look in his eye. A woman in a white lab coat, focused and intent. A little girl standing in front of a house in Chicago. A young woman dressed in fatigues keeping watch from behind a corner in a burned out house. An adult woman dressed to the nines strutting across the driveway of a swanky hotel and getting into a limousine.

And then another. Rachel recognized herself, but the image was blurred. She was sitting at the head of a long table in a poorly lit room. Other forms, mostly men, sat around the table. One stood at the other end of the table, addressing the group. Somehow, Rachel knew that she was the person the others were looking to for…something. But what?

It dawned on her. The father? Hers. The elderly woman? Her grandmother. The woman in the lab coat, her mother. And she was the little girl. The "view" was her. All at once.

Rachel closed her eyes, trying to absorb what she'd seen.

Mr. Randal stirred. "Rachel, it will be hard; hard to hold on, hard to climb, hard to let go. Know that you are not alone."

## Chapter Sixteen

# THE CALM BEFORE

G rayson touched her hand again, this time to escort her to the elevator. Mr. Randal and the other three stood as she rose from her chair, silently wishing her all that is good, and for her to carry a heart of courage moving forward into her future. At least that's what Rachel felt as she walked toward the door: an overwhelming sense of good intentions toward her.

The doors closed. Grayson was silent. Rachel's head spun with wonder and confusion mixed with a giddy hopefulness. It was a completely irrational state of mind, yet seemingly appropriate. After all, she'd just witnessed an illogical, nonsensical peek of life across something boundless. A forever time, yet deeper than that. Her logical mind was having none of it, but her soul had found an opportunity to speak, and speaking it was.

The doors opened to the lobby. "Good evening, Mr. Raphael," the doorman said.

"Good evening, Robert. How are you this evening?"

"I'm well, sir. Thank you for asking. The driver will be here any minute. You're welcome to wait in the sitting area and enjoy some coffee or tea. I just put a log on the fire."

Grayson looked at Rachel to ask if she was interested.

"Sure, why not?" Rachel asked. "Some hot tea sounds good to me."

"Well, all right. Yes, Robert. We'll take you up on that. Thanks," Grayson said.

Grayson prepared two cups of Ginger Peach tea and sat down across from Rachel. "Do you want to talk about it?" he asked.

Rachel looked up at Grayson and grimaced. She wasn't ready to talk about it. "About what? I mean, which part?"

"Any part you want. I'm here to support you, remember?"

Rachel thought back to their conversation. He was her *grace given*. "I know you are. I'm okay, really. It was just a lot to take in...all at once." She smiled, chuckling at her choice of words.

"What's so funny?"

"Get it? A lot to take in all at once?"

"I don't get it."

"Come on, Grayson," Rachel said, suddenly not so sure he knew what she was talking about.

"Look, I don't know you very well, and I don't know what you saw in there, but your face...it was so different. It's like you left."

"What do you mean it's like I left?" Rachel asked.

"It just seemed like you were somewhere else. I don't know. It was as if you were taken up into something."

"Grayson, did you hear Mr. Randal ask me to look around? I did. Didn't you?"

"Sure I did, but I didn't notice anything unusual."

Rachel was puzzled. He was right there and he didn't see it. "Grayson, I can't explain it, but I will say this: the group of four functions above and outside of our continuum of time and space. But you knew that."

"Yes, I know that. What I'd like to know is what you saw."

"Let me put it this way. I told you about the data readout display, right? It gives a single transcendent all-encompassing real-time view of all the data transmission activity across the globe. Technically, that's not possible."

"Okay…I'll take your word for it. Go on."

"So…what I saw in there was like the data readout display, but on steroids. Major steroids."

The doorman walked up to the sitting area. "Mr. Raphael, the driver is here to pick up your guest."

"Thank you, Robert. He must have gotten stuck in traffic."

"I don't think so, sir. He made very good time. It was exactly ten minutes ago that he called to say he would be here, and as you can see by the clock, he's right on time."

Grayson looked at Rachel and smiled. "Of course, what was I thinking?"

Grayson walked with Rachel out to the main lobby area to meet Peter. "I have a limo lined up for tomorrow morning. I've asked that we be at The Kimberly at 7:00 am," Grayson said.

"That seems a little early, doesn't it?"

"Not if we want to stop for coffee and conversation before-hand," Grayson said.

"I look forward to it."

~

"*I*t was my pleasure to drive you, Ms. Wheaton. Really! I had time to hang out with my friends and make my dad happy, all at the same time," Peter said.

"Yes, there's a lot of that going around," Rachel said.

"Pardon me, Ms. Wheaton?" Peter looked confused.

"Oh, nothing Peter. I'm glad you were able to make good use of the time. We got a lot of work done today, and your willingness to come pick me up made it easier."

Peter pulled the town car up to the front of The Kimberly.

"Don't bother, Peter. I can get out," Rachel said.

"I insist," Peter said, as he quickly exited the vehicle and came around to the passenger door. "Have a good evening, Ms. Wheaton."

"Thank you, I will. Goodnight." It was cold outside. Rachel made a quick dash for the lobby hoping to stop at the fire for a few minutes, only to find the lobby filled with people, a bunch of business types attending some kind of reception.

Feeling around the bottom of her bag for the room key, she remembered she had new digs to look forward to. The room had not one, but two fire places. Excited to spend some time exploring her new temporary home, she headed straight to the bank of elevators, slipped into one that was empty, and took a long leisurely ride to the 28the floor. The doors opened up to the quiet and seemingly empty floor, the hallway enveloping her with a cozy sense of safety. She'd be able to relax tonight.

~

*R*achel startled to wakefulness at the sound of the room phone.

"Yes?"

"Good morning, Mrs. Hancock. This is your wake up call."

*Hancock? Oh…right.* "Amir? Is that you?"

"Yes, Mrs. Hancock. Good morning. It's 5:45 am, your regular time for a wake up call."

"Thank you, Amir. Um…Amir, would it be possible to get some fresh coffee delivered to my room?"

"Certainly-"

"By you?" Rachel asked.

Amir paused for a sliver of a second. "Yes, ma'am, that can easily be arranged. Is there anything in particular you'd like? Latte or cappuccino? Regular brew?"

"How about a nonfat latte with sugar free hazelnut flavoring?"

"Excellent. What size?"

"The largest size you have. And please bring some Sweet n Low."

Right away, Mrs. Hancock. I will make the arrangements and be there by 6:05," Amir said.

"Thanks Amir. See you soon." Rachel hung up the phone and popped out of bed. She'd slept well, probably because of the 1800-thread count sheets. The room was temperature controlled, soundproofed, and equipped with automatic window shades that rose at the first hint of sunlight. The en suite was massive, equipped with a large glassed in shower, claw-foot tub, sauna, and a to-die-for walk-in closet. Time for some music to get ready by.

*Lenny sounds good.*

Rachel felt confident about the day. Even the shower delivered at the perfect pressure and temperature. *Are You Gonna Go My Way* blasted from the sound system as she washed her hair, her singing voice sounding ten times better given the acoustics of the en suite.

Jumping out of the shower, she wondered if they'd prepared enough the night before. Did they have a clear pitch? She didn't know. Maybe they should just stick to the original scope and only propose the team. Take it one step at a time. If they got there and it was obvious they could move more aggressively, she had the option to do that. Grayson didn't know what she'd been considering, so no risk of confusion there. The plan depended upon Amir anyway. She'd talk with him when he arrived. Then she'd know what her end game possibilities were.

Amir would be knocking on her door soon, so she got dressed before starting her makeup. As for her hair, it would have to be a curly day; no time to blow-dry and flat iron. She needed something though.

One of the vanity drawers was half-open. She reached over to shut it and noticed a sparkle peeking out from inside. She opened it to find a gold hair brooch. Suddenly the en suite was awash in a golden light.

*How convenient. Wow...what a sparkle.*

It was the perfect solution for taming her unruly mane. She brushed her hair out and formed a modified French twist, securing it in the back with the brooch. Thinking it might look a little too elaborate for a business meeting, she took one last look in the mirror.

*Uh-mazing! Too yummy to pass up.*

There was a knock on the door. Rachel turned *Lenny's* volume down and went to check the peephole, but the door didn't have one. She looked around and discovered a monitor on the kitchen counter. The screen was divided into four quadrants, three displaying changing views of all the hallways on her floor, and one unchanging display of the suite's entrance. Amir stood there waiting with a beautiful silver tray containing coffee and breakfast pastries.

Rachel laughed and opened the door. "Amir, please come in."

"Good morning. It's nice to see you. I brought some goodies to go along with your coffee," Amir said.

"Yum! Would you join me? Or at least stay for a few minutes? I need to talk with you about something."

"Absolutely, Rachel. Like I said before, whatever you need. And if you don't mind me saying so, you look radiant."

"Thank you. That's very kind. Why don't we have a seat in the living room? And by the way, thank you for this gorgeous room. I'm feeling very spoiled right now."

"It's my pleasure, Rachel. What would you like to talk to me about?" Amir asked.

"Yesterday I had a chance to more closely review the access reports you'd given me, and I have a few questions. If I understand the data correctly, I should be most interested in the keycard ID as a means of identifying the individuals who accessed the room, right?"

"That's right. With only one exception, each of us carries a master keycard with a unique ID assigned to us. The number in the ID field should tell us who it was that entered."

"What's the exception?"

"There's a small pool of unassigned cards kept for the house-keeping staff. We sometimes use contract staff to fill in when we're busy. They're not assigned a specific keycard. Instead, they're provided with one of the pool cards. The system doesn't pick those up."

"That seems like a design flaw."

"Our HR system is a little older. Keycards can only be assigned to people who are in our HR system, and contractors aren't entered. They're tracked manually right now."

"That's not good."

"Why's that?"

"I went through the report and eliminated all the entries I could account for as my own. That left three to review. The first one I noticed occurred during late morning. No keycard ID for that one. The second one occurred in the afternoon. It was the cleaning crew. They were here for over an hour-"

"That's too long…"

"Wait…yes, I know. They were here for an hour and they unpacked my luggage and put everything away. I mean, the room was perfect when I got there. The good news is that there's a keycard ID. I'm going to need your help in researching who it's assigned to."

"Of course, that shouldn't be a problem. I'll work on that today."

"You rock. Okay, so the last one is a bigger mystery than the other two. There's an entry at 5:45 am, no key card ID. Both this one and the one in the late morning were situations where it looks like the door was held open for only a few seconds, and then closed. As if someone opened it, held it open, did whatever they did in a matter of seconds, and then left, closing the door behind them."

Amir looked pensive. "Hmm. That's very strange." He seemed to be trying to sort out how that might have happened.

"What is it? What are you thinking?" Rachel asked.

"Well, the afternoon access makes a little sense except for the length of time. The late morning access could have been a contractor, but your theory about someone holding the door open makes me suspicious. I can't think of any reason why that might happen, but I'll check it out with housekeeping."

"What about the third one?"

"That's the one that's troubling me. Housekeeping doesn't start operations until 6:30 am, which is 45 minutes later than when the access occurred. I'm not sure I can help you with that one. I can at least see if they had a contractor keep a key overnight. That's not allowed, but we don't always get the keys back before they leave for the day."

"Amir, that third one is the most important one to research, okay? You understand?" Rachel looked hard at Amir, trying to convey to him that the 5:45 entry was the highest priority of the three.

"Yes, ma'am. I'm on it."

"All right…that's that. Now, there's one more thing I need to talk with you about."

"I'm all ears, Rachel."

## Chapter Seventeen

# AND SO IT BEGINS

"I should be back later this morning. You have my cell, right? And I've programmed your number so I'll know to pick up," Rachel said, mentally reviewing the list of items they'd discussed.

"I'll be awaiting your call-"

"Oh, I almost forgot. I won't have my cell with me today. If we do an offsite today, Mr. Raphael and I want to be sure we can't be tracked. I guess I'll have to contact you the old fashioned way, eh?"

"I'm sure I will find that to be most refreshing," Amir said, smiling ear to ear.

"All right, my friend. Au revoir."

"Speaking French now, are you? Very nice."

"It must be the new digs," Rachel said, chuckling. "You go now...I know you're late," she said, waving him away while closing the door.

"Have a good day, Mrs. Hancock," Amir said.

The door clicked shut. Even though she'd be leaving soon, Rachel locked both the top and mid-door bolts. It was time to pull herself together before meeting Grayson out in front of the hotel. Today was easier. She had no doubt about the security of the room, except...

*The brooch...*

Grabbing her cell, she dialed Amir's number.

"This is Amir."

"Amir, one last thing. I found something in the room this morning. I need to know who stayed here last, and I need to know if anyone accessed the room last night while I was in Tribeca."

"Got it. I'm on it. I'll also pay attention to the access activity today. In fact, I'll tell housekeeping to contact me when they're ready to service the room."

"That would be fabulous. Thanks so much."

"You're welcome. "

The brooch, as lovely as it was, had changed things again. She'd hoped to secure the key case in the room safe. Now she wasn't sure leaving it behind was such a good idea. Yet, today wasn't the day to carry it on her person. Despite Trader and Priestly's efforts to put on a good show of healthy corporate culture and harmony, she and Grayson were entering a hostile environment. Somebody knows she has the case, and maybe it's one of them. She couldn't take it with her; too risky. The room safe was her only option. She'd have to trust Amir to do what he said he would.

*R*achel stepped off the elevator and started walking through the sitting area and into the main lobby. People were looking at her.

*Whud ya lookin' at?*

She was feeling extraordinarily upbeat, and a little sassy. Not her normal disposition under the kind of circumstances she faced. A few people abruptly stopped dead in their tracks as they caught her walking by.

*Okay, what's going on? Did I forget to button my blouse?*

Rachel looked down, slyly felt around her back to check her skirt, and confirmed all was in place. Deciding to ignore the stares of strangers, she made her way directly through the front entrance doors where Charles was talking with a guest just outside.

"Yes sir, you're all set," Charles said as the guest got into a cab. He turned to greet Rachel. "Good morn...ing, Ms. Wheaton." He was clearly taken aback.

"Good morning, Charles. Beautiful morning, isn't it?" Rachel asked. "You seem a little startled to see me. Were you not expecting me?"

"Oh yes, I was expecting you. But I wasn't expecting *you!*" he said.

"You too, huh? I swear, I don't think there was one person in the lobby who didn't stop and gawk as I walked by. What? Do I look like an ogre or something?"

"No, Ms. Wheaton. On the contrary, you look extraordinarily stunning. Striking. I can't put my finger on it. Maybe it's your hair. Is it different today?"

"Oh gosh...it can't be my hair. It's an unruly mane. I didn't have time to tame it, so I had to pin it up with a brooch I found in the en suite. I kind of like it, though."

"Well, if you don't mind me saying so, it suits you well," Charles said, grinning with his goofiest smile so far.

"Thank you, Charles. Is the car here yet?"

Right then, a limousine pulled up.

"Yes, Ms. Wheaton. Right this way."

The limousine slowed to a stop. Rachel could see Grayson waiting for her inside. Charles opened the passenger door, motioning for Rachel to take her seat on the passenger couch.

"Have a wonderful morning, Ms. Wheaton," Charles said as he gently shut the door.

"Good morning, Ms. Wheaton," called a voice from the driver's seat. Rachel looked up to see who it was. Peter looked into the rearview mirror to greet her, but his expression suddenly changed. It was as if he'd seen a different person.

"Good morning, Peter. You look a little rattled. Is everything all right?"

"Uh, yes ma'am. Everything is fabulous!" Peter said.

"Good morning, Mr. Raphael," Rachel said as she turned to her limo companion.

Grayson stared back.

Something was wrong. Something was very wrong.

"Mr. Raphael, is everything all right?"

Grayson was looking at her as if he didn't know who she was.

"Michael? What's wrong?"

"My apologies, Ms. Wheaton. There is something different about you today. I can't quite put my finger on it, but it seems familiar."

Rachel thought he was joshing her. "Oh come on, what do you mean? Familiar in what way?"

"You may not want to hear this, but you remind me of my mother."

# COPYRIGHT

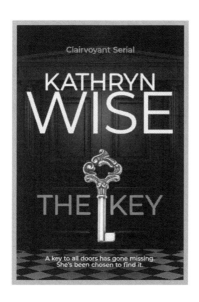

In the off chance you haven't read *The Key*, the first installment of the Clairvoyant Serial, you really must read it before
you start *The Clock*. I want you to fully enjoy *The Clock*…
that's why I'm offering you *The Key* FREE.

## FROM KATHRYN WISE

## Download My Book!

# ENJOY THIS BOOK? YOU CAN MAKE A DIFFERENCE

### Leave a Review

Reviews are the most powerful tools in my arsenal when it comes to getting attention for my books. Much as I'd like to, I don't have the financial muscle of a New York publisher. I can't take out full page ads in the newspaper or put posters on the subway. (Not yet, anyway.)

But I do have something much more powerful and effective than that, and it's something that those publishers would kill to get their hands on.

**A committed and loyal bunch of readers.**

Honest reviews of my books help bring them to the attention of other readers.

If you've enjoyed this book I would be very grateful if you could spend just five minutes leaving a review (it can be as short as you like) on the book's Amazon page. You can jump right to the page by clicking the link above.

Thank you very much.

# ABOUT THE AUTHOR

Kathryn Wise is the author of the Clairvoyant Serial. She makes her online home at www.KathrynSWise.com. You can connect with Kathryn on Twitter at @KathrynSWise, on Facebook at https://www.facebook.com/authorkathrynwise and you should send her email at kathryn@soul-words.com if the mood strikes you.

# ALSO BY KATHRYN WISE

*In the Clairvoyant Series*

*The Key*

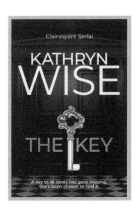

**A key to all doors has gone missing.**
**She's been chosen to find it.**

Social media has moved far beyond photos, favorites, and follows. Hidden behind the innocent screens of unsuspecting users, its ubiquitous tentacles grow increasingly integrated across tech companies, leaving little room for anyone; individuals, companies, and governments; to remain free from its overreaching global grasp. Now one sinister force wants to take full control.

But Rachel Vaughn is a bad ass. And she works for the good guys.

An escalating pattern of unexplained social media outages triggers the call for her expertise in data forensics and special ops, setting her on a hunt for an algorithmic key with the power to take down the entire global infrastructure.

Day 1 in Manhattan begins her odyssey of dangerous and otherworldly encounters, including her first contact with special ops agent Grayson Blaine. With him by her side, she prepares for what may become her most dangerous assignment yet. The enemy is vehement in their quest, hindered only by the absence of one important puzzle piece; a piece that only Rachel can provide.

*The Key* is the first installment of the five-book *Clairvoyant Serial* by Kathryn Wise, an eclectic thriller you won't be able to put down. Don't wait...and then move straight on to the next installment, *The Clock*.

∿

*The Clock*

**It no longer keeps time. It defies it.**

Time is running out.

Massive social media outages wreak havoc while the world demands a remedy. Service is quickly restored with each incident, but the windows of relief are short-lived. As long as the algorithmic key remains in the wrong hands, the outages grow in their reach and frequency across the globe, threatening to hamper the world's major economic regions and disrupt the societal stability of the world.

Rachel and Grayson move quickly, assuming undercover personas as part of a plan to infiltrate the enemy. The target of their charade? An upstart social media company: the prime suspect behind what could become a devastating global debacle.

Day 2 begins and Rachel's strategic intuition is tested when she finds herself pitted against an unexpected corporate adversary; an adversary with both an acquired taste for relentless power, and shocking ties to others too close for Rachel's comfort. As she and Grayson navigate the unexpected twists and turns of their mission, the second hand ticks on.

*The Clock* is the second installment of the five-book *Clair-*

*voyant Serial* by Kathryn Wise, an eclectic thriller you won't be able to put down. Don't wait...find out what happens next and then get ready for *The Hunt*, coming in the early Fall of 2018.

*The Other Books in the Serial*

There are three other books in the serial, but since Kathryn "writes into the dark," even she doesn't yet know exactly how each story will unfold. She only has a sense of the metaphorical backstory on each, which of course she must keep to herself for now. You still want a hint? Check out the book covers here.

Printed in Great Britain
by Amazon